—High Tea—
LOW OPINIONS

A Tea & Sympathy Mystery

BOOK 8

J. NEW

High Tea Low Opinions
A Tea & Sympathy Mystery
Book 8

Cover design: J. New.
Interior formatting: Alt 19 Creative

Introducing 'New Friends' on Facebook –
Join the Conversation.
Keep up with the latest
giveaways, new releases, and more.
facebook.com/groups/1857000347910602

OTHER BOOKS BY J. NEW

Chapter One

*L*ILLY TWEED, FORMER agony aunt with the local newspaper, now purveyor of fine teas at The Tea Emporium in the small northern English town of Plumpton Mallet, jogged across the car-park at the back of the market square. She was on the way to the Agony Aunt's cafe, which she part-owned with her former nemesis, now very good friend Abigail Douglas, to pick up lunch for herself and her shop manager Stacey, and she'd just seen a large coach pull in, packed to the gills with visitors wanting to spend their holiday money in this historic town. It was one of the official tour groups. The town was popular with visitors all year round, but the spring and summer months saw an increased influx, which no other town in the north of England could match. So much so that there were days when the tourists out numbered the residents by five to one.

The reason for her current and uncharacteristic physical exertion was the fact her shop was one of the main tour stops, and her young American manager was on her own. She leant against a nearby wall, grabbed her phone from her pocket and called the shop.

"Hello," she puffed out, once the girl had answered.

"Hey! Watch it, you creep. Go get your kicks somewhere else!"

Lilly would have laughed, but she didn't have the energy or the breath.

"Stacey, it's me," she gasped out.

"Lilly, is that you?"

"Yes."

"What are you doing? I thought you were a heavy breather!"

"Jogging. Hang on, let me just get my breath back."

"Jogging?" Peals of laughter reached Lilly's ears.

"I know, I know. Believe me, I wouldn't be doing it if it wasn't necessary. A leisurely cycle to work and jogging, actually make that sprinting, from one end of the town to the other are completely different disciplines."

"What's so urgent?"

"There's a tour group just turned up. They'll be in the square shortly and heading your way." Lilly could hear rustling paper as Stacey checked the calendar.

"But they're not on the schedule for today. I've been really careful to make sure all the dates are listed, so we have adequate cover."

"I know. They must have changed the itinerary and forgotten to tell us. Will you be okay for ten minutes while I nip to the cafe and get our lunch?"

"Sure, no problem. I'll find some way to entertain them. Maybe juggling?"

Lilly choked out a laugh. "Well, as long as you're not juggling cups and saucers or spinning plates, that's fine. See you in a bit."

"Sure. And maybe walk back, okay? I don't want you passing out in front of the customers. It's bad for business."

Lilly was still chuckling when she entered the cafe. Abigail popped up from behind the counter and slapped her forehead when she saw her.

"Oh no, Lilly, I forgot to get your lunch order ready."

"Don't worry. I'll wait for my turn like everyone else. You're busy, I take it?"

"I've been on my feet all day, every day, for the past week. Look at this!" she said, lifting the cuff of her linen trousers to reveal ugly swollen veins. Lilly grimaced.

"Oh, Abigail."

"I know. Varicose veins! Aren't they awful?"

"And painful I expect?"

Abigail nodded morosely. "I'll have to see the doctor, I suppose. But I can't afford to take time off if I need an operation."

"Good grief, Abigail, don't be daft. Of course you can. Your health comes first. We can switch the rotas round no problem. I think you should sit down for a minute. Fred will sort my lunch order out."

"Already doing it, Lilly," Fred called out from behind the counter.

"But we're so busy."

"I hate to break it to you, but you're about to get busier. I've just seen a tour coach in the car-park."

"What?" Abigail squeaked. "I didn't think they were coming for another couple of days."

"Neither did I. So sit down and get some rest while you can. Have you got anyone you can call to cover this shift?"

"I've just given two servers and a barista a couple of days off, so they'd be back for the rush on Friday," she moaned. "I really should have run that by Stacey, but I was trying to be an understanding boss. Well, it's the last time I'll do that."

"Do you need me to help?"

"No, we'll manage. You need to help Stacey today if there's a load of tourists just arrived. But if you could help at all tomorrow and Thursday, that really would be a lifesaver."

Lilly nodded. "I can do that. I'll have a chat with Stacey and see who can cover the tea shop while I'm here."

"Thanks, Lilly. So, have you got the call yet?"

"No, not yet. But you'll be the first to know when I do."

Fred waved, indicating her take out lunch was ready, and he'd also prepared two tall iced coffees for them.

"That's great, Fred, thank you. Abigail, I'll see you later."

As predicted, when she arrived back, the tea shop was full thanks to the tour group and Stacey was busy with customers. Luckily, there was no juggling. Lilly quickly put their lunch and drinks under the counter and began to work the shop floor while Stacey brewed tea samples and dealt with the sales.

"These are new, Lilly," the tour guide said, pointing to the porcelain white teacups with gold rims and the shop logo on the side in gold.

"Yes, they are. Stacey designed them. They make great souvenirs. Look at the reverse."

Lilly turned the cup around to reveal a beautiful monochrome line drawing showing a scene of the market square and the shop.

"Wow, that's gorgeous. Your manager really is talented. You ought to do place mats and coasters with this design. I'll take one, please, Lilly. And one of those fabulous ceramic kettles shaped like a teapot. The one with the colourful beach huts. It reminds me of my childhood holidays."

After an extremely busy hour, in which Stacey and Lilly sold more tea sets, tea boxes and miscellaneous items than they could ever remember in one day, the tour group trickled out en route to the next stop on the agenda, and Stacey and Lilly finally had time for their lunch. Lilly smiled at Earl, who, realising it had all gone quiet, returned from the storeroom where he'd been hiding and resumed his spot in the window.

Lilly was half way through her pasta when the shop phone rang.

"The Tea Emporium."

"Hello, can I speak to Lilly Tweed, please?"

"Speaking. Can I help?"

"Oh, hello, Lilly. It's Laurel Flowers here."

"Laurel, how nice to hear from you. How can I help?"

Lilly beamed. This was the call she'd been waiting for. The one Abigail had asked her about earlier. Stacey caught her eye, grinning and giving two-thumbs up in response to hearing the woman's name.

"I was given your name by Lady Defoe, as you're probably aware?"

"Yes, she did mention I might hear from you. You're looking to cater for a fundraising event as part of the re-election campaign for Mayor Goodwin, I believe?"

"That's almost right. The event is to raise funds for the town officially, although Mayor Goodwin is also hoping to be re-elected again this year. To be honest, I'm calling to officially book you and your team. Lady Defoe has been waxing lyrical about your food and capabilities. As have some others I've spoken to. It seems pointless therefore for me to look any further when I obviously have the best business for the job in my own town. Can we arrange a meeting to talk about it in more detail?"

"Of course," Lilly said, grabbing the diary and swiftly turning the pages. "How is Friday for you?"

"Ah, no good, I'm afraid. The working week is always chock-a-block. I have Saturday at two o'clock free. Would that suit you?"

"Yes, that would work perfectly," Lilly said. If necessary, she'd re-arrange her whole diary in order to get this particular job. "Do you want me to come to your office?"

"Actually, I'd rather hoped we could meet at your cafe, if that's convenient?"

"I'll ask Abigail to reserve a table for the three of us. Is there any particular tea you'd like?"

"As a matter of fact, Lady Defoe sent me a box of your summer strawberry blend recently and it was sublime."

"Summer strawberry it is. I'll put a box aside for you as well," Lilly said, glancing at Stacey, who was busy scribbling notes.

"That's very kind, thank you. I'll send you an email with my thoughts so far, and we can discuss it further on Saturday."

"I look forward to meeting you," Lilly replied. Then said goodbye and ended the call.

"Did we just book the mayor's fundraiser?" Stacey asked hopefully.

"We did!"

She quickly phoned Abigail to give her an update, and even Stacey, who was at the other end of the counter, could hear her squeals of delight.

"Well done, Lilly," Abigail said. "Now, I need to go and sort out which treats will best complement the strawberry tea. See you later."

Lilly was ecstatic. This would be their biggest and most high-profile event yet.

Chapter Two

*T*HE REMAINDER OF the week flew by and before Lilly knew it, she was walking down to the cafe for the meeting with Laurel Flowers. With no private bookings for that day, Abigail had already set up the tea room in preparation. She would have liked to be able to open up the room for any walk-in customers as Saturday was usually very busy, but this event was an important one so she closed it off for the duration of the meeting and made sure it was looking its absolute best for Laurel Flowers.

"I must admit, I'm very excited about this event, Lilly. It could be the beginning of something huge for us if it all goes well."

"I agree. It's going to be a lot different to catering book clubs, the odd wedding and birthday parties, though."

"But we can do it, partner!" Abigail said, clapping her hands together in undisguised glee and excitement. Lilly laughed and nodded. "I'm just going to check the oven. I've got the pastries and scones in for Laurel to sample, and heaven forbid I burn them. I won't be a minute."

While Abigail was in the kitchen, Lilly set out the binder she'd put together full of ideas Laurel could look through and pick and choose as she wanted. Half an hour later, they were all seated, sipping the summer strawberry tea.

"Gosh, I've been craving this. It's not addictive, is it?" Laurel asked with a smile.

"No, don't worry. You can't get addicted to it, but it's definitely moreish," Lilly said.

"You can say that again. Do you sell it here at the cafe, too?"

"We do," Abigail replied. "Although we've put a box aside for you."

"That's very kind. Thank you, ladies. I'll try not to drink it all at once."

"It's very good cold over ice with lemonade or sparkling water and a sprig of fresh mint too."

"Gosh. I think I need to really stock up. That sounds like a great idea for a summer garden party, Lilly."

Laurel Flowers was a very attractive petite woman in her late-thirties, with an elfin face and large, dark blue eyes under a short mop of curly blonde hair. She reminded Lilly of Tinker Bell in the Peter Pan stories. But she knew the woman had a steel core and didn't suffer fools gladly. Considering her job as the mayor's right-hand woman, she expected that sort of temperament would come in handy. It wouldn't do to underestimate Laurel Flowers. Lilly felt she'd be a stickler for detail, with a need for things to be perfect. They'd really have to pull out all the stops if this event was to be a success. She'd turned up wearing a stunning silk jumpsuit in deep turquoise, which both Lilly and Abigail admired.

"Thank you. It's from my mother's range. She owns a small chain of luxury women's boutiques in London. I have the matching lingerie, too," she said with a wink. "Now," she said, replacing her empty cup on the saucer and pushing it to one side. "I'm pressed for time, as per normal, so let us get down to business. I appreciate you getting the quote to me so quickly, Abigail. However, the numbers have almost doubled since we last spoke. Mayor Goodwin has been glad-handing door-to-door recently and has also done a couple of public events, all of which have worked like a charm. Many have bought tickets to the event who otherwise wouldn't have done so. Will that be a problem?"

"Goodness me, no," Abigail said, before Lilly had a chance to say the same thing. "We're more than capable of handling the increase."

"Excellent. If you could get the revised quote to me as soon possible, I'll get the deposit organised."

As Laurel talked about what her expectations were for Mayor Kenneth Goodwin's annual fundraising event, Lilly began scribbling notes and working out the logistics. They'd already assigned the staff, but with the event doubling in size, it would mean training new staff members, which would take some time. In all probability, it would also mean closing both the cafe and the tea shop for the afternoon. But, the increased revenue for the fundraiser would more than cover those losses. Luckily, the tea room they were currently in wasn't booked on the event day.

Laurel was explaining what decor she had in mind when her phone rang. She glanced at the caller ID and let out a frustrated sigh.

"Sorry, I need to take this or he'll just continue to pester me."

She got up and moved to the far side of the room. But with only the three of them present, both Lilly and Abigail had no problem hearing Laurel's side of the conversation.

"Carl, I'm in a meeting. Can't this wait? Of course we were serious about the invitation. Why on earth wouldn't we be?" There was a pause while she listened. "Oh, for heaven's sake, Carl, don't be so ridiculous. Tell Councillor Davis we both look forward to seeing him. Goodbye." She abruptly ended the call and returned to the table.

"Sorry about that."

"Is everything all right, Laurel?" Lilly asked.

"Yes, it's fine. That was Carl Bates, Councillor Davis's nephew. An irritating thorn in my side. Russell Davis, in his foolish wisdom, has taken Carl on as his new assistant. I don't know if you're both aware, but Councillor Davis is running against Mayor Goodwin this year and seems to think Carl can help him win," she scoffed.

"Someone has put their name in the hat this time?" Lilly asked in surprise.

"Is that unusual?" Abigail asked. Not being from Plumpton Mallet originally, she wasn't au fait with the town's elected officials.

"Mayor Goodwin is extremely well liked in Plumpton Mallet," Lilly said. "He's a local and passionate about the town and its residents and is very fair. He's done a lot to increase tourism and highlight local environmental issues, as well as care for both the elderly and youngsters alike. And improvement to local services. I'm really surprised someone is running against him. I don't think that's happened in the past four or five elections."

"He's been our mayor for that long? I thought the elections were every four years?" Abigail said.

"Exactly. It just proves how popular he is."

"Thank you for that glowing endorsement, Lilly. I happen to agree with you, but Councillor Davis believes he has a good chance of winning," Laurel said now. "And frankly, it pains me to admit it, but he just might. He's not a bad choice. He's young and energetic, and that is attractive to people. I actually quite like Russell Davis, although he can be a bit single minded and acerbic on occasion. Particularly if you don't agree with him. But his nephew..." she tapered off and sighed again.

"Is he really that bad?" Abigail said.

"Strictly between us, he's like a child. He's extremely competitive and, as far as I can gather, will do anything it takes to ensure his uncle is elected. I wouldn't put it past him to get sneaky and underhand as the deadline draws nearer. Obviously, as I'm Mayor Goodwin's assistant, Carl has decided he and I are in competition with one another and he will not leave me alone. I sent an email inviting them to our fundraiser. This is normal practice. We invite all the councillors to our events and they do likewise. Russell, as a member of the town council, has always attended and wouldn't dream of not coming to this one just because he's running in opposition to Kenneth. But Carl seems to think it was some sort of joke. He's not politically savvy. Actually, he's a bit of an idiot, if I'm honest."

"I'm sorry he's making things so difficult for you," Lilly said.

Laurel waved the comment away. "I'll deal with it. It's part of my job. I'm not complaining, really. Now, let's get back to the event. The strawberry tea is a definite, but I'd like to give the attendees some other options. Certainly the lemon lavender one, which I've tried and like very much."

"It's our most popular blend to date," Lilly said, making notes.

"I've set out several samples here," Abigail said, switching on the kettles.

"Thank you, Abigail. Now, let's talk about the food."

The meeting lasted close to two hours, much longer than any of them were anticipating. But, with an event as important as this one, it needed to be right, and Laurel, as Lilly had predicted, was indeed a stickler for detail. With everything on the list ticked off, and Laurel had said goodbye, Lilly and Abigail discussed the sharing of various tasks.

Abigail would get the revised quote together and send it to Laurel along with the invoice for the deposit. It would include additional equipment, staff and training, as well as an assortment of sundry items like tablecloths and centrepieces.

"My main concern is the staff training," Abigail said. "Cafe and tea shop skills are fine, but we're looking at silver service for this and none of them are up to scratch."

"We'll have to do this after hours, Abigail, and I think we'll have to offer bonuses for doing so."

"Good idea. I'll see if I can add it to the invoice. In an ethical way, of course. I got the feeling Laurel would be quite happy to pay for this sort of thing, actually. She really does want us on board. So, what about some sort of additional incentive for them? Say, a special dinner for everyone who signs up?"

"I like it," Lilly said, making a note. "I know it's very last minute, so we're bound to have some who can't do it, but the bonus and dinner should appeal to most of them. I'll get Stacey to contact them and arrange the schedules. Two nights this week for additional training should be enough, but if any are having issues, then we can do some extra."

"That shouldn't be a problem."

"Right, I need to get back to the tea shop. Give me a ring if there's anything you need. See you later, Abigail."

Chapter Three

*L*ILLY, ABIGAIL, FRED and Stacey met outside The Tea Emporium early on Monday morning. They had a meeting with Laurel at the venue, and as it was the quiet time in both businesses, Stacey had organised replacement staff.

As the four of them set off to walk the short distance to the King's Hall and Winter Gardens, Stacey asked about the building.

"It's a beautiful building, isn't it?" Lilly said. "Grade II listed, and is a complex of public buildings. The Town Hall is at the centre, then on the left is the library and the tourist information office, and on the other side is the King's Hall and Winter Garden theatre. The library, Town Hall and King's Hall, opened in 1908 and the Winter Gardens was added to the west in 1918."

"Wow, how do you know so much?" Stacey asked.

Lilly shrugged. "I love my town. And we had to learn about it when I was at school. I know, I know, it was a long time ago," she said in answer to Stacey's grin. "But some things just stick."

"You know, you might be interested in the library, Stace," Fred said.

"Oh, why is that?"

"Because it's a Carnegie library. The funds were donated by your fellow countryman, Andrew Carnegie."

"Really? Wow! You're right, that is interesting. Hey! I've got more in common with this town than I realised. That's so cool. So all the council offices are above?"

"Only above the Town Hall, tourist information and library," Lilly said. "The rest of the buildings have an upstairs."

"In the Winter Gardens they hold all sorts of events," Fred said, taking Stacey's hand as they crossed the road from the market square. "Book sales, art exhibitions, coffee mornings. Everything really. And the King's Hall puts on plays and bands and that sort of thing."

"Has anyone famous played here?" Stacey asked.

"Loads. It's a really popular place for bands as part of their tour dates. Comedians too. The county music festival has been held here since it opened."

"I must say, Fred, you're also very knowledgeable about these buildings," Abigail said.

"It's my town, like Lilly said, and I love it too. Besides, I remember most of it from my school's local history lessons, too. They've been teaching about the local history ever since the school was built, I think."

"Here's another bit of interesting history for you," Lilly said. "It has been the location for various rallies in the past. Including ones addressed by the suffragette Adela Pankhurst, William Booth of the Salvation Army, and Robert Baden-Powell."

Stacey shook her head in awe. "Man, the history of this place is amazing. I had no idea."

"Neither did I, Stacey," Abigail said. "I feel rather privileged that we're catering an event in such an esteemed building."

"Here we are. I hope you like the inside as much," Lilly said, just as the clock in the turret of the Town Hall next door struck nine o'clock.

❧❧❧

*L*ILLY LED THEM up the stone steps and into the small foyer, where she opened the door to the King's Hall proper. Inside, they found Laurel on the stage at the far end of the room, pacing back and forth while talking animatedly on the phone. She looked up at the sound of the door banging closed, and gave a quick wave, indicating she would only be a minute. A moment later, she bounded down the steps and joined them on the main floor.

Lilly introduced Fred and Stacey and after Laurel had thanked them for coming so early, informed them Mayor Goodwin would like to meet them.

"Are you setting up already?" Stacey asked. The concertina doors separating the two venues had been fully opened and she could see tables being maneuvered into position.

Laurel smiled. "No, that's not for us. These buildings are always booked well in advance. I believe this is for the local WI chapter. They have a large meeting tomorrow."

"WI. What is that?" Stacey asked Abigail.

"The Women's Institute. It's an organisation set up in the 1900s. It was started to revitalise rural communities and encourage women to be more involved in producing food during the first world war. It's a stellar organisation, and all voluntary. They looked after the evacuees during the second world war, too. There's a lot of information at the library and the historical society, I believe, if you want to know more."

"That's really interesting. Thanks, Abigail. Are you a member?"

"Not yet, but I'd like to be in the future. At the moment, with the cafe being in its infancy, I need to concentrate on that."

Lilly could see Mayor Goodwin talking with a couple of men and Laurel waited until he had finished before approaching to introduce them. Lilly didn't know him personally, but had attended a memorial garden he'd opened in the local park a few years before. He'd changed since then, putting on some weight and losing much of his hair. But he was still genuinely friendly and affable.

"Laurel, I was told Luke Moore wanted to speak with me again this morning. Is he coming here?"

"Yes, he's on his way."

The Mayor smiled, satisfied, then turned his attention to Lilly and the others.

"You must be our catering team. From The Tea Emporium and The Agony Aunt's Cafe, have I got that right?"

"You have. I'm Lilly Tweed, and this is my business partner, Abigail Douglas. We're very pleased to have been chosen to cater your event, Mayor Goodwin."

"I'm glad to hear that," he said, shaking their hands. "And who are these two?"

"Stacey Pepper and Frederick Warren."

"A pleasure. And as we've all been introduced, please call me Kenneth. I attended the recent memorial at the rowing club, albeit briefly, and had the pleasure of tasting your food and drinking your tea there. Lady Defoe was the one who recommended you, I believe, but having seen for myself what you can do, it seemed fitting to have you cater for the event. I prefer to deal with and support local businesses whenever possible."

"Laurel said you're expecting quite a crowd this year?" Lilly said.

"It's always that way during election year. Everyone wants to attend. Although, this year has seen the highest number of attendees yet, which I'm very pleased about. Oh, while I remember, Laurel, Davis confirmed his attendance with me directly, so you can add him and his guests to the list."

Laurel nodded and pulled out her tablet and began tapping.

"Lilly, Abigail," she said. "I'll email you the updates now, but it won't change the numbers. I'd already included Councillor Davis and his party."

"And this is why she's the best PA I know," Kenneth Goodwin said. "I'm glad she's on my team and not the oppositions."

"Isn't Councillor Davis your rival?" Stacey asked.

"Oh, I didn't realise you were an American. You're a long way from home, Stacey. What brings you to Plumpton Mallet?"

"I'm only half American, actually. My dad's a Brit. But, I'm a student. I'm studying Sports Therapy at the university."

"Well done. Our university is one of the best in the country. And yes, to answer your question, Russell Davis is running against me this year, but this event is a fundraiser for the town. There are various community initiatives that need a cash injection. That said, it is great PR for the election, but nothing we raise here will go towards my re-election campaign. Russell is a fellow Councillor and we all attend these events. In fact…"

But whatever Mayor Goodwin was about to say was halted by a shout from the other end of the room.

❦❦❦

"**M**AYOR GOODWIN! MAYOR Goodwin!" a frantic voice shouted as its owner strode across the room.

Luke Moore was a local and a regular at Lilly's tea emporium. He owned an award-winning butcher shop in a small hamlet half an hour's walk from the town.

"Mr Moore," the Mayor said, holding out his hand.

"Did you get my emails, Mayor?"

"I did, Mr Moore, and I'll try to put your mind at ease. I'm going to do my very best to get re-elected. But, on the off-chance I'm not, I seriously doubt Councillor Davis's redevelopment plans will go ahead. There's just not the budget available for what he has in mind, and believe me, there's already a lot of opposition to the idea of demolishing the buildings in that area. I'd like to reassure you that your business will be safe, whether I'm the mayor or not. I'm still a member of the council and will fight to make sure you're treated fairly, no matter what ideas my competitor has."

Luke Moore let out a shaky sigh.

"Thank you, Mayor."

Kenneth Goodwin grasped Luke Moore's shoulder.

"Why don't we take a walk and discuss your concerns in more detail? Laurel, can you handle things here?" Laurel nodded. "All right," he turned to Lilly and the others. "It's been a pleasure to meet you all. No doubt I'll see you all again on the night. Now, if you'll excuse me." Mayor Goodwin escorted Luke away.

Lilly turned to Laurel.

"Does Russell Davis want to knock down Luke Moore's shop?" She was stunned anyone would even suggest such a thing, let-alone run a mayoral campaign on the back of the idea.

Laurel rolled her eyes.

"Not just the butcher shop, either. The whole row. He needed a policy for his manifesto, and that's one of the ideas he chose. I mean, he has a point when he says the buildings are an eye-sore and not in-keeping with the rest of the town's historical look. They were built in the seventies. Goodness only knows how they got planning permission in the first place. But, his plan would put the council so far in debt we would never dig ourselves out. They won't approve the idea and realistically Russell knows it, but it's something to talk about during his campaign."

21

"But that's nuts," Fred said. "Who's going to vote for someone who wants to get rid of one of the best loved shops we have? That place has been around since before I was born and they do the best sausage rolls and pork pies anywhere. I mean, it's a mile away, so it's not as if it's close to the town centre. What difference does it make if the building isn't of historical significance? It's what's inside that counts. It's part of the community."

"Wow, well said, Fred," Stacey declared, gazing at her boyfriend in admiration.

Laurel agreed.

"Perhaps we should take you on as part of team Goodwin," she said with a wink, causing Fred to blush to the roots of his hair. "I'll take you to the rear of the premises now so you can see what you have to work with. It's a full catering kitchen, so you shouldn't have any problems."

They all trooped after Laurel, who walked as fast as she spoke, and entered the large kitchen at the back of the venues. Lilly and Abigail glanced at one another and nodded in unison. This would do very nicely.

Chapter Four

IT WAS THE day of the event and Lilly had just laid the last of the cloths on the table, while Abigail was right behind her, positioning the blue and white central floral arrangements they had designed for the occasion. They'd decided on a type of conveyor belt system, which was working extremely well. Behind Abigail came Stacey, laying the main plates, Fred with the side plates and James, Stacey's father, who was up from London visiting his daughter, laying the cutlery. Other staff were following on with the cups and saucers and glassware.

"I can't believe how much Stacey has learned in your shop over the last year," James said to Lilly, the note of parental pride in his voice unmistakable. "Who would have thought she could put together a combined high tea and afternoon tea with such skill?"

"You have a very bright daughter, James. I'm very lucky to have her. And Fred, for that matter. They work very well together. Don't you think?"

James watched Stacey and Fred for a moment, then nodded.

"Yes, they do. He also treats her as an equal and with respect."

Lilly was sure Fred had heard the comment but didn't let on. It had taken a while for James to come round to the fact his daughter was growing up and dating. He'd not been a fan of Fred initially, but Lilly realised he was just being overprotective. It wasn't really Fred he had an issue with. It would have been the same with any boyfriend Stacey had chosen. Having not been a part of his daughter's life for so long, he'd had trouble relinquishing the reins to start with. It was still a work in progress, but he was doing much better at giving Stacey the space she needed and accepting her choices.

As James moved to another table, Fred sidled up to Lilly with a smile on his face.

"I heard what he said. Maybe he does like me after all?"

"I'm sure he does, Fred. It's just taken him a bit of time to come to terms with the fact that Stacey is not the child he remembered."

Fred returned to his job, polishing each plate thoroughly before laying them, and Lilly stood back, casting a professional eye over the tables, looking for anything out of place or that jarred with the whole effect. She was just moving a cup and saucer on the table to her right when someone came up and grabbed her round the waist. She let out a yelp and spun round.

"Archie! Good grief, you gave me a shock. What are you doing here?"

Archie laughed and gave her a quick kiss on the cheek, suddenly mindful of the room full of staff. Most of whom were smiling indulgently at his affectionate antics.

"I thought you might need some help. See, I even donned my working togs," he said, turning in a slow circle to show off his jeans and tee-shirt, both of which looked brand new to Lilly. She could see the fold creases in his shirt. He'd obviously put it on straight from the box. "But I can see you've got everything under control. I must say, it looks very impressive."

"That's kind of you, Archie. But yes, we've almost finished. How about I make you a cup of tea and pepper you with questions instead?"

"Sounds intriguing. Let me guess, you want all the sordid details of my misspent youth?"

Lilly laughed. "Absolutely! But we'll save that for another time."

Ten minutes later, while Abigail and the team had moved to the kitchen, Lilly and Archie sat on the edge of the stage with cups of lemon lavender tea.

"So, what is it you want to know, Miss Tweed?"

"Do you know anything about Russell Davis's intentions if he becomes mayor? And anything about his family?"

After Laurel had told her about Carl, Lilly was anxious to know more about the candidate running for mayor in opposition to Kenneth Goodwin.

Archie frowned and rubbed his chin.

"Well, I haven't written about any of them."

"That's a good thing, considering you're a crime reporter."

"Indeed. To be honest, I've only heard what's currently the talk on the grapevine. And I suspect you've heard the same thing. Namely, he has intentions to knock down a row of well known and well loved shops on the outskirts of town."

Lilly nodded. "Yes, I'd heard the same thing. Although Mayor Goodwin doesn't think he stands a chance."

"I hope he's right. There' are a lot of the residents, myself included, who rely on some of those shops."

"So, you don't know anything about Russell Davis's family?"

"Only that his sister's son has been taken on as his assistant. Russell and his sister seem to have a good relationship."

"No gossip about Carl?"

"Nothing I can think of. Why all the interest, Lilly?"

Lilly shrugged.

"I just wanted to know a bit about the person running in opposition to Kenneth Goodwin. I thought you might know a few things us mere mortals aren't privy to."

Archie grinned. "I can't think of any juicy tidbits off-hand. But I shall keep my ear to the ground just for you. If I find out anything, I'll let you know. We meet up as part of a crowd on the odd occasion, so if he lets anything slip I'll pass it on. Now, if you don't need me, I must go home and change into something more suitable for this shindig. I can't have Plumpton Mallet's crème de la crème seeing me dressed like this."

Lilly laughed. Archie was always impeccably dressed, even in his so called 'working togs.'

*A*N HOUR LATER, the guests had started to arrive. There was already a bar in situ at the premises, and Laurel had hired the local brewery to run it, so, unless people preferred cups of tea, there was no need for her services until they all sat down to eat. Everything was under control in the kitchen so Lilly got changed into her waitress outfit then took time to walk around the main room. Casting yet another critical eye over the tables. Laurel's fastidiousness had her triple checking everything.

She spied Archie, glass of champagne in hand, and walked over to greet him.

"You look wonderful, Archie," she said, inordinately pleased to see he had paired his charcoal grey suit with the waistcoat she had gifted him on their steam train trip.

"Why thank you, Miss Tweed. I must say you're looking particularly fetching yourself. I do like that frilly white apron. You look like an old-fashioned nippy. You must wear it more often," he said with a ridiculous gleam in his eye.

Lilly grinned. "That's enough of that, Mr Brown. So, do you know everyone here?"

"Most of them. There's the mayor with his assistant, and some of the other council members, at the bar. Councillor Davis, the opposition, with his nephew are over there, talking to some of the town's elite and other members of the council staff."

Lilly didn't recognise the majority, but one person was very familiar.

"Lady Defoe is with him."

Archie nodded. "I'm not sure who the others are, but no doubt they are some more of our wealthy residents. While Mayor Goodwin is adamant, this fundraiser will bring the town together, you can be sure the majority of the attendees are the cream of the crop. You really do have to be someone to get an invitation."

"I'm not so sure about that, Archie. The young couple just being served both work out of town. They've been to my shop numerous times and I've heard him complaining about the early morning commute. Particularly when the trains have been cancelled due to leaves on the line or some other nonsense."

Archie grinned. "Well, perhaps some of the middle class have sneaked in, like myself."

"Rubbish. I know for a fact you received an invitation. Anyway, there's nothing wrong with being part of the working classes. Where would the town be without us? You'd be sitting down here with nothing to eat, for a start."

"Quite right. I was just pulling your leg."

"I know that. I also know that additional tickets to the event were sold on a first come, first served basis. Laurel told me how successful the mayor's door-to-door was, so the event is open to those that genuinely want to come and support him and raise funds for Plumpton Mallet in the process."

"Indeed. Ken is always very fair to everyone, no matter what walk of life. It's nice to see so many of the residents have attended. Just proves how popular he is and how much they all love the town. As well as a jolly good knees-up, of course."

Lilly laughed. "Yes. Any excuse for a party. If you don't mind, Archie, I'm going to take the opportunity to go and talk to Russell Davis before I get too busy. I have some questions I'd like to ask him."

Archie nodded, and after a quick peck on her cheek, left to join the group from the Plumpton Mallet Gazette. Lilly wandered over to where Councillor Davis was holding court.

"And then he told me the fish was too small," Russell Davis said, and his companions burst out laughing. Lilly had obviously walked in on the tail end of a joke. The young couple excused themselves and Lilly took their place next to Lady Defoe.

"Hello, Lilly. How are you? I must say, I'm looking forward to seeing what delights you and Abigail have for us this evening."

The two women made small talk for a couple of minutes, then Lady Defoe went to mingle and Lilly found herself in front of the Councillor and his nephew.

"Councillor Davis, I wonder if I might talk to you for a moment?" she said.

"The Councillor is busy at the moment," Carl said, eyeing Lilly's outfit with undisguised derision. He'd obviously pegged her as someone of little importance. Lilly was shocked at his rudeness but stood her ground. As not only a local business owner but a member of the voting public, she wanted a few questions answered.

"Now, Carl, this is a community event," Russell Davis said. "The least I can do is talk to... I'm sorry I didn't catch your name."

"Lilly Tweed. I own the Tea Emporium and The Agony Aunt's cafe in town. I'm also catering for this event."

29

To her surprise, Davis laughed and turned to his nephew. "You see, Carl, one thing you must never do is upset the chef. Not unless you want to find something horrible in your food. Isn't that right, Ms Tweed?"

It was a poor joke and Lilly chose not to answer. Neither she nor Abigail were in the habit of adding nasty things to the food of customers they didn't like. It would never even cross her mind to do such a thing. She smiled thinly.

"Actually Councillor..."

"Russell, please."

"I was wondering, Russell, what your plans are for the town and the local businesses if you are elected?"

"Well, that's a simple question to answer. I want to put our beloved town on the map. I want to build up the town so we get more tourists and increase our local economy. There are many improvements that can be made and I plan on doing just that."

"But how are you planning on improving Plumpton Mallet? We already get many tourists, particularly during the spring and summer months. And that number is increasing all the time. As my businesses are both part of the tour stops, I have it on good authority that it's likely the tour companies will be stopping here daily in the near future. Also, now the Christmas market has been added as a much bigger event, we're seeing a lot of tourists during the winter too. I feel as a community we're doing very well in that regard."

"We could always use more revenue, Lilly. I want this town to grow much bigger. We have plenty of room outside of the main area for new developments. Much of it is an eyesore and won't be missed."

"Like my shop, you mean?"

Lilly turned and came face-to-face with the butcher, Luke Moore. He had an angry gleam in his eye and Lilly's heart sank. The last thing they needed was trouble.

Leeee

*L*ILLY TOOK A forced step back as Luke Moore launched into a tirade, not more than a foot away from Russell Davis's face. Suddenly, Carl pushed his way between them.

"Back off," he growled.

"Not until he admits he's going to destroy my shop and the other businesses on the outskirts of town," Luke growled back. "And destroy our livelihood! That shop has been in my family for generations. What gives you the right to demolish it?"

Several people had moved closer now to listen and gawk. While Councillor Davis had a smile plastered on his face, Lilly could tell he was extremely uncomfortable at being confronted by Luke Moore. Carl put a hand on the butcher's chest and pushed him away from his uncle.

"Don't you touch me," Luke said, and returned the push.

Carl was shoved straight into Russell, who staggered back against a table, upsetting the carefully placed glasses, his face turning red with anger.

"Start acting like a civilised human being and I won't have to," Carl countered.

"I'm not the one trying to ruin our town," Luke shouted. "What's civilised about ruining people's lives?"

"If you don't leave my uncle alone, it won't only be your shop that's destroyed," Carl threatened, clenching his fists.

Russell came to stand beside him, both looking ready to fight. The argument was escalating quickly and was about to get violent. With perfect timing, James Pepper appeared with Mayor Goodwin and Archie, with Laurel just behind. The Mayor stepped forward.

"All right, let's calm down, shall we? This is neither the time nor the place for such appalling behaviour."

James took Luke gently by the arm and he and Archie persuaded him to walk away. Lilly mouthed a thank you to them. Archie nodded and gave her a quick wink.

"Remember, this is a fundraiser for the town. To bring the community together not tear it apart," Goodwin said to Davis.

"Did you hear what Moore was saying about Uncle Russell?" Carl said.

"No, I did not. But this is not the place for a fight," Kenneth Goodwin replied, steel in his voice and his face like thunder.

"Ken is right, Carl," Russell said, putting a restraining hand on his nephew's arm. "As my wife says, we want to make a good impression. There's a lot riding on this little shin-dig. We need to make sure we've got these people on our side."

As the Mayor left, tasking Laurel to set up the podium ready for the speeches, Carl and Russell were joined by a smartly turned out woman.

"What are you two up to now?"

"Just a slight misunderstanding, Felicity. Nothing to worry about. I was just reminding Carl what you said about good impressions."

Felicity Davis kissed her husband's cheek and told him to remain calm. "We're trying to convince people to vote for you, darling, not brand you as a thug and scare them away. Good publicity only, remember?"

She turned to Lilly and introduced herself. "You must be, Lilly Tweed. I've just been speaking to Lady Defoe, and she informed me you were catering today. Russell and I have both been to your cafe and enjoyed it very much. I'm looking forward to what you have in store for us this evening."

"Thank you," Lilly said. "I think I might be to blame for that spot of trouble. I was asking your husband what his plans were if he was elected."

"It wasn't your fault. You're perfectly entitled to ask him about his propositions for the town. Anyone is. Luke Moore would have approached Russell whether you'd been there or not. My husband is very proud of his ideas and has put a lot of thought into them to minimise the disruption and loss of earnings it will have on the business owners. I'm quite sure he'll be able to bring more revenue into Plumpton Mallet whilst ensuring it's a town united, not divided," Felicity Russell said.

She should be running for Mayor, Lilly thought. She was poised, knowledgeable, articulate and certainly looked the part. She also appeared to have an innate ability to keep the peace. Or at least keep her husband and nephew under control.

The two women chatted for a moment longer, with Felicity asking for Lilly's number to put in her phone. She possibly had a personal event coming up and would like to use Lilly's business to cater for it. With the conversation over, Lilly righted the glasses that had been knocked over during

33

the unpleasantness. Miraculously, none had been broken. She then made her way to the kitchen with the thought that with his wife by his side, Russell Davis might have a real chance of winning the election. Before she joined Abigail and Stacey, she approached Archie and asked how Luke Moore was.

"He's calmed down a bit, but he's still convinced Russell is going to tear down his business. He's joined a few friends, so let's hope he remains calm for the rest of the evening. I'll keep an eye on him, don't worry. But, I must say, Lilly, if those really are Russell's plans, then he'll not be getting my vote."

Chapter Five

ITH THE SERVING underway, Lilly watched from the sidelines and was pleased to see everything was running smoothly. Drifts of conversation about how wonderful the food was reached her ears, and she felt a warm glow of a job well done. Abigail would be thrilled to know her selection of both open-and-closed artisan sandwiches, the individual quiches and miniature salmon en-croute were being received so well.

At one point there looked to be a potential squabble for the last puff pastry pizza twist, but a waiter with his eye on the table deftly laid a new three tier stand packed to the gills with delectables.

Lilly nodded and returned to the kitchen.

"How's it going out there?" Abigail asked, elbow deep in soapsuds.

"Couldn't be better. Stacey, you did a fantastic job of training everyone. Not one of them has made a mistake. They really are on the ball. And, more to the point, they look as though they're really enjoying the experience."

Stacey shrugged. "They were easy. What's that English saying you guys have? They took to it like a fish to water?"

"Duck," Abigail and Lilly said in unison.

Stacey hit the floor. Abigail and Lilly burst out laughing.

"Oh, my god, that's the funniest thing I've seen in ages," Lilly said, wiping the tears from her eyes.

"What's going on?" Stacey asked, rising slowly and poking her head above the table's edge.

"The saying. It's duck not fish."

Stacey grinned. "Oh, right. I thought you were telling me to hit the deck for some reason."

James walked in with two empty tea pots.

"We need fresh pots of the strawberry and lemon lavender, please. And most people are ready for the scones, jam and cream, now. The speeches are underway. Stacey, what on earth are you doing on the floor? Are you all right? Have you hurt yourself?"

Stacey giggled. "Never mind, dad. I'm fine. Just a misunderstanding. I need to brush up on my English idioms, that's all."

"I see," James said. Although he didn't at all.

With the pots replenished and on their way to the appropriate tables, servers clearing away the main courses and, beginning with the final one, Lilly returned to the event room to keep a watchful eye on progress. A second later, a waitress asked if she'd mind taking over for a moment while she used the bathroom. Lily agreed and moved over to her section, realising it was Russell Davis's table she'd been serving. Felicity was absent, but Carl and his uncle were in deep conversation. She took a pot of tea and began to refill the cups.

"I told you, Carl, I will talk to your mother later," Russell hissed.

"But I need to know now what you're going to do about it," Carl insisted, with a distinct whine in his voice. "It's hardly fair, is it?"

"I don't know. But if you continue to push me, I'll not help either of you. Now, let that be the end of the matter."

With the waitress returned, Lilly took a position by the wall, wondering what the argument had been about. Obviously, it had something to do with Carl's mother, the sister of Russell. But, according to her last conversation with Archie, the two of them were supposed to have a good relationship. She was itching to ask Archie about it, but he was enthralled with Mayor Goodwin, who was currently nearing the end of his final speech, so she returned to the kitchen as the event was nearing its end.

"I think the mayor is just about finished," she told Abigail and Stacey. "Well done. I believe bonuses and a bit of a party for our terrific staff are in order. I think we can safely say it's been a success."

"It has," Kenneth Goodwin said from the kitchen door. "The food and the service were superb. Better than many a five-star restaurant I've dined at in our capital. I'll certainly be recommending you in the future. Many thanks for all your help, ladies."

"You're very welcome," Lilly, Abigail and Stacey said.

"I'd better return to my guests. Thanks again."

Lilly followed him out, ready to help clear the tables once the guests had risen. It didn't take long and finally the only job remaining, while the guests were milling about chatting and saying final farewells, was to remove the tablecloths and shake them outside the back door.

"I'll do those, if you like?" Jill, one of the part-time staff, said as they reached the kitchen.

"Thanks," Lilly replied, handing the bundle over and moving to help Abigail pack up their clean crockery.

A second later, she was back in floods of tears and talking incoherently. Lilly dashed over.

"What is it? Are you all right? Jill, take a deep breath and tell me what's wrong."

"There's a body out there," the girl choked out. "I think it's Mr. Davis."

꘎ꔆꔆꔆ

"OH, DEAR LORD. Not again," Abigail said, plonking herself down in a chair at the kitchen table and putting her head in her hands. "We're cursed."

Lilly looked at her friend and privately agreed. She asked Stacey to take care of Jill while she ventured outside. Hoping against hope the girl had got it wrong.

She hadn't.

She took out her phone and immediately called her detective friend Bonnie to explain what had happened. After a few shocked expletives and a similar comment to Abigail's, she gave Lilly instructions to keep everyone in the building. She was on her way.

"Tell only those you need to, Lilly," Bonnie said. "No one else. And don't let anyone mess up the crime scene. I won't be long."

Lilly returned to the kitchen to find Abigail was back to packing up the dishes and Stacey was encouraging Jill to drink the hot sweet tea she'd made.

Abigail turned when she entered.

"Is it true?"

Lilly nodded.

"Yes, I'm afraid it is. I've called Bonnie. She's on her way. I need to tell the mayor what's happened, but, if we can, this must remain a secret until the police arrive. Can you make sure no one goes out the back? And no one can leave the building."

Abigail nodded and Lilly, after taking a deep breath to calm the anxiety, went to find Kenneth Goodwin. He was with Laurel, so she took them both to one side and told them what had happened. Both looked completely stunned, but after a minute or two Laurel went into business mode, and suggested the mayor make an announcement explaining that everyone would need to remain for the time being due to an unfortunate accident.

Kenneth nodded and turned to Lilly.

"What happened?"

"I don't know. We'll have to wait for the police to arrive. The main thing is to keep people calm and ignorant for as long as we can. We'll make pots of tea and coffee and begin to serve them, but I would suggest you close the bar. I don't think anymore alcohol is a good idea."

"Yes, I agree. Laurel, could you do that while I make the announcement?"

Laurel nodded.

"Yes, of course."

As expected, after the mayor's announcement, there was a clamouring from the guests asking what was going on. He promised answers as soon as he had them, but asked that they return to their tables for the moment and drinks would be served shortly. The guests complied, but Lilly knew if the enforced incarceration went on for too long, people would begin to get frustrated or even angry. She hoped Bonnie would arrive before that happened.

On her way back to the kitchen, Archie fell into step beside her.

"What's going, Lilly?" he whispered. "I saw you speaking to Ken and Laurel just before his announcement. Is it serious?"

Lilly took his arm and in the quiet hallway outside the kitchen told him what it was all about.

"Good grief! Dead? I can't believe it. Was it you who found him? Are you all right?"

"It was Jill, one of the waitresses. Stacey is looking after her. I'm okay, Archie. Although in complete disbelief like you are. Could you go back in there and try to keep the peace until Bonnie arrives? I need to go and guard the crime scene. And keep your eyes peeled for anything unusual. One of those people in there could have done it."

"Are you saying he was murdered?"

Lilly nodded.

"I think he might have been. I wasn't there long enough to notice the details, but I have to go back. Could you go and eavesdrop a bit, Archie?"

"Of course," he said, drawing her in for a fierce hug. "Hang in there, Tweed," he whispered. "We'll sort it all out. Don't forget, I'm only in the next room if you need me."

"Thanks, Archie."

Returning to the kitchen, she found James had taken Jill to the adjacent office. It was quiet there, and the girl was in terrible shock. She told Abigail tea and coffee would be needed again for the guests, and her friend, ever the professional, immediately started unpacking teapots, cups, and saucers. Jumping at the chance to do something useful to keep her mind off the awful circumstances.

With everything in hand, Lilly returned to the crime scene. She didn't venture further than the door, but she noticed something she'd missed previously. It looked as though Russell Davis had been stabbed. She glanced around as much as she could without moving her position, but could find no sign of a weapon. Then she suddenly thought about Felicity. Someone needed to inform her about her husband. She dashed back to the main room and found Kenneth talking to her softly. She was carefully dabbing her eyes with a lace-trimmed handkerchief. It looked as though Carl had also been told. He was standing still, a look of utter shock on his grey face.

A beep on her phone found a message from Bonnie saying she and her team would be there in approximately five minutes. She returned to the body and what felt like the longest five minutes of her life.

Chapter Six

SIX MINUTES LATER Bonnie was at her side, staring down at the inert form of what had, not long ago, been a living, breathing, human being.

"If it wasn't for you," she began. "Me and my team wouldn't have anything to do."

"Don't you start," Lilly said. "Abigail thinks we're cursed."

Bonnie snorted. "She could have a point there. I think I'd have a quieter life if I went to work for the Met."

"You'd go straight to the top position, Bonnie. You've certainly had enough practice."

Bonnie smiled and nodded. Then her face turned serious. The necessary banter was over.

"Thanks for preserving the integrity of the scene."

"Unfortunately, I've had enough practice, too."

"Who found him?"

"Jill. One of the waitresses. She's in the office just off the kitchen. James is looking after her. She's in shock, Bonnie."

"I'd be amazed, and highly suspicious, if she wasn't. All right, I'll speak with her first."

"It should have been me who found him. I was about to come out to shake the tablecloths when Jill offered. So, what do you want me to do?"

"I'll need to speak with everyone who was here tonight."

Lilly nodded. "I'll let Mayor Goodwin know. He'll probably make an announcement. Is that okay with you?"

"As long as he keeps it vague. No mention of the murder. Although the way this town works, I wouldn't be surprised if they all know, anyway. I'll catch up with you later."

"Okay. I did notice he appears to have been stabbed, but there's no sign of a weapon."

Bonnie patted her shoulder.

"Thank you, Miss Marple. I'm sure my crime scene technicians and the pathologist will value your insight."

Lilly smiled.

"I'll get out of your hair."

Back in the main room, Lilly found Kenneth and Laurel and drew them to one side, repeating what Bonnie had said. A moment later, Mayor Goodwin was back on stage. He tapped the microphone a couple of times and the room went silent as hundreds of pairs of eyes swivelled in his direction.

"Ladies and gentleman, thank you for your patience. I've just been informed that the police have arrived and will want to talk to you all individually. While I'm not able to give you any additional information at this time, please give them your help and support. Thank you."

There were a couple of groans, but most people remained seated and began to speak in hushed tones. With nothing for her to do, Lilly joined the serving team, dispensing tea and coffee. She noticed Lady Defoe was comforting Felicity Russell in a darkened corner of the room, and Carl was with a group of people nearer his own age, all of whom were providing comfort and support to the shocked man. She'd be very surprised if the remainder of the guests hadn't put two and two together and realised something serious had happened to Russell Davis.

She walked across the room and approached Felicity, asking if she could get her anything. She declined but asked Lilly if she could please find Carl. She wanted to be with her family. Lilly turned to find Bonnie had entered the hall and had already begun talking to the guests. She moved in the direction of where she'd seen Carl last, but he was no longer there. Casting an eye around the room, she saw him duck out of the main door into the foyer.

She swiftly approached Bonnie and told her she'd just seen Carl leaving. The two of them hurried out of the building and caught up with him in the station car-park opposite.

"Where do you think you're going?" Bonnie demanded.

"$\mathcal{I}$ NEEDED TO GET some air," Carl said. "I've just been told my uncle has been killed. I was shocked. I suddenly couldn't stand to be in a room with so many people. I had to get out of there before I had a panic attack."

"Even though you knew everyone had officially been told not to leave the building? That I was in the process of questioning all those in attendance?"

"I was overcome with grief and couldn't breathe," Carl insisted, tears running down his face. He stopped speaking and pulled a handkerchief from his pocket, blowing his nose noisily. "I'm sorry I left, but I couldn't bear to be in the room any longer. I needed some space and privacy before I lost it. It was like the walls were closing in and the air was thickening." He waved a frustrated hand. "I can't explain it properly. Have you ever lost someone close to you so suddenly? Like, one minute they are there, then the next they're gone. For ever. It's paralyzing and overwhelming."

Lilly watched Carl intently. She couldn't quite tell if he was genuinely upset or had just been determined to get away from the police. He'd been very close to his uncle, so the grief was most likely genuine. It certainly looked and sounded legitimate. However, she'd heard them arguing just before Russell Davis had been killed. Had Carl stabbed him in a fit of anger, and the now shock and tears a result of him suddenly realising what he'd done? She couldn't be sure.

"Well, as I still need to speak with you, I'll do it here," Bonnie said, extracting her notebook. Carl nodded and shuffled over to a wall close to a fire engine red Toyota. He sat down heavily. Shoulders stooped and head bowed.

"Ask away. I've nothing to hide," he mumbled.

"Where were you sitting for the event?"

"With my aunt and uncle."

"And where were you when your uncle's body was found?"

Carl frowned. "In the room, of course. Where else would I be?"

"Did you leave the main room at any time?"

"No. I was there to help support my uncle in his bid for mayor. It was my job to stay there and talk to people. He needed me by his side to explain his ideas for improvements to Plumpton Mallet, answer any questions and allay any concerns they may have had. He had a run in with one of the other guests, though. Do you know about that? We almost came to blows at one point. He's the one you should be questioning."

Bonnie made a note. "So, you were in the room the entire time talking to the guests? Which means any of those people should be able to account for your whereabouts during the whole event, correct?"

"Actually, I did leave. Just once, to answer my phone," Carl said.

"Who was it who called?"

"My mother."

Bonnie made another scrawl in her book.

"I can easily verify that. Did you leave the room for any other reason?"

Carl shook his head. "Not that I can recall. I've told you, it was my job to be at my uncle's side, and that's what I did."

Carl was becoming antagonistic and sarcastic and Lilly was finding it increasingly difficult to be sympathetic towards him. She could see Bonnie was feeling the same.

"Is this your car?" Bonnie asked, abruptly changing tack and indicating the red Toyota.

"Yes."

"Where did you buy it?"

"What's that got to do with anything?"

"Answer the question."

"I didn't, okay! If you must know, my uncle bought it for me. As his personal assistant, he felt it would look better if I had a good car. I was representing him wherever I went. I could hardly turn up in an old banger, could I?"

Bonnie made another scribble, then asked Carl how things had been between him and his uncle before he died?

"Things? What do you mean, things?"

"Were you getting along? Any arguments or differences of opinion?"

"There was a bit of an issue, but it was a family thing and has nothing to do with his death. I had absolutely no reason to kill my uncle, if that's what you're insinuating," Carl said forcefully.

"What was the issue?"

"None of your business." Bonnie glared at him and raised an eyebrow. Carl quailed slightly but stuck out his chin. "My uncle and I were on the best of terms. The argument was no big deal."

"If it wasn't a big deal, then you can tell me all about it, can't you?" Bonnie replied, with an edge to her voice Lilly recognised. She was beginning to lose patience.

"I don't want to talk about it. It has no bearing on this crime."

Bonnie remained silent for what seemed, to Lilly, like the longest time, just staring at him, then nodded.

"I'd like to look in your car," she said.

Carl hesitated for a moment.

"My car? Why?"

"Because it's my job. Can I have your keys?"

Carl sighed loudly and, after getting off the wall and standing, thrust his hand in his trouser pocket.

"Fine," he said. He searched his pockets with mounting exasperation. "I'm always losing the stupid things," he said crossly. Eventually, he found them in his inside jacket pocket and put them in Bonnie's waiting hand.

Bonnie unlocked the car, opened the driver's side door, and leaned in. She pulled her head out quickly and strode over to Carl.

"Carl Bates, you're under arrest for the murder of Russell Davis," she said, snapping the handcuffs around Carl's wrists.

"What? No! I didn't murder my uncle."

"Then maybe you can explain why there is a bloody knife in your car?"

⋆⋆⋆

LILLY GASPED, AND Carl's eyes widened in complete shock.

"Is this a joke?"

"Do I look as though I'm joking, Mr Bates?" Bonnie said.

"I swear I don't know what it's doing there! I didn't murder my uncle. You must believe me! Someone else must have put it there. The real murderer. I'm being set up. Please, I swear I'm innocent."

Bonnie read him his Miranda rights and told him to save any comments for the formal interview when his solicitor was present. She radioed for two PCs to come over. The first to collect Carl and take him to the station, the second to guard his car. Then contacted a crime scene technician to collect the knife and impound the Toyota for examination.

Once the constable had arrived and taken Carl away, and the other was in place on guard duty, Lilly followed a determined Bonnie back to the King's Hall, where she immediately approached Mayor Goodwin and drew him to one side.

"Mayor, I need to make an announcement."

"Of course, detective. The podium is all yours."

He led her to the stage and after checking everything was switched on, Bonnie approached the microphone.

"Ladies and gentleman, thank you for your patience. As you are no doubt aware, Councillor Russell Davis died this evening. We have good reason to believe he was murdered, and I'm now able to tell you we already have a suspect in custody."

As expected, the room erupted with noise as people shouted out questions and demanded to know exactly what had happened and who'd been arrested. Several of the women burst into tears, and two fainted. Bonnie folded her arms and remained still. Waiting patiently for the furor to cease and for the crowd to slowly calm down, while she took the opportunity to observe the room and its guests carefully. Eventually, when it was quiet again, she cleared her throat and spoke.

"I'm not able to comment or answer any questions with regard to an ongoing investigation. However, myself and my officers will need to speak to everyone individually in order to take statements. They will be coming around shortly, so please make yourself available. Thank you for your patience. That's all."

Bonnie left the stage and approached the mayor. Felicity joined them a moment later and asked Bonnie where Carl was.

"Perhaps I could have a word with you both in private?" she answered.

Lilly watched them leave, knowing she was going to break the news that Carl had been officially arrested for the murder of his uncle.

"Lilly," Laurel said, joining her. "Thank you for everything you've done this evening. It's been a dreadful end to what was a promising fundraiser."

"It has. Are you all right?"

Laurel smiled grimly.

"As long as I don't think about it, yes. If I remain detached, I can do what needs to be done and get through it. Once I get home, the seriousness of the situation will probably hit me. But I can't afford to think about it now."

"I understand. Is there anything more we can do for you here?"

Laurel shook her head. "Everyone wants to leave after they've given their statements to the police, so you may as well start to pack up now."

Lilly nodded, said goodbye and returned to the kitchen where, after she'd been told Jill had gone home as Bonnie had already spoken with her, she was immediately peppered with questions from Stacey and Abigail.

"So you won't tell us who killed Russell Davis?" Abigail asked, busy making up Tupperware containers of the extra food for the staff.

"I can't, Abigail. It's up to Bonnie to make the announcement. The investigation has only just started and I really don't want to put my foot in it. Someone has been arrested, as you know, but honestly, that's all I can say."

"It's okay, we understand," Stacey said. "Right, Abigail?"

"Of course we do. Although, I expect Lilly already has her deerstalker at hand."

Lilly smiled and shook her head.

"Oh no I don't. This time I'm leaving it to the police."

Chapter Seven

THE NEXT MORNING Lilly awoke bright and early, knowing there was a lot to do at the shop. When she'd finally got home the previous evening, she'd found Earl on the sofa. Fast asleep on his back with a paw across his face. He'd looked so cute and peaceful she hadn't wanted to disturb him. She'd crept upstairs and fallen asleep within minutes.

At some point during the night, Earl had joined her and curled up at the bottom of the bed. Now, as she came to, she felt his weight and discovered she had pins and needles in both feet.

As she hopped and stamped about the bedroom, trying to bring back the feeling, Earl stretched and raised his head, giving her a perplexed gaze.

"Next time, I'll go to sleep on your paws, Mr Grey," she said, scratching his one and a half ears as life began to return to her feet and ankles, and the pins and needles diminished to a slight itch.

Washed, dressed and breakfasted, she and Earl set out on the bike for the scenic journey to work. At the shop, she found Stacey was already putting away the services they'd used for the event.

"Morning, Lilly. How are you doing?"

"Morning, Stacey. I'm fine, thanks. What about you?"

"Yeah, I'm okay," she said, bending to stroke Earl before he disappeared to his basket in the window.

"I still can't believe how the event ended yesterday," Lilly said, grabbing a couple of plants to display on the bike outside.

Stacey nodded glumly.

"Me neither. Did he do it, do you think? Carl, I mean."

"Oh, you found out it was him Bonnie arrested."

"It was obvious really, as he was the only one missing. Anyway, I overheard Felicity talking with the mayor and put two and two together. So, do you think it was him?"

"I honestly don't know, Stacey," Lilly replied, going outside to arrange the floral display. She turned the shop door sign to open and moved behind the counter to put the kettle on. "I'm leaving it to Bonnie and the police. How are you really?"

"Honestly, I'm fine. I was busy in the kitchen all the time, so missed everything. And I never went out the back."

The door bell tinkled and a couple of customers entered. The next hour was a rush of brewing, demonstrating, selling and packing up customer items. Then, just after ten o'clock, the bell chimed again and Archie walked in. The latest edition of The Plumpton Mallet Gazette was tucked under his arm.

53

He greeted them, removed his hat and coat, and after a quick peck on Lilly's cheek, took a stool at the counter.

"A 'hot-of-the-press' personal delivery of the paper for you lovely ladies," he said. "I was up all night getting it together. Have you got any energy tea? I'm in dire need if I'm to function at all today."

"I'll brew you some liquorice root, Archie," Lilly said. "And add some lemon and honey. That should do the trick."

While the tea was brewing, Lilly glanced at the paper. The front-page headline came as a bit of a surprise. It wasn't strictly about Russell Davis's death, but the fact that his wife was now running in his stead. A large, official, professional portrait photograph of Felicity took up most of the space, but it was more of an announcement than an article.

"I didn't realise Felicity Russell had decided to run. Isn't it a bit soon?" Lilly asked Archie. "Surely she should be taking time to grieve?"

Archie shrugged. "I've not been able to get a quote from her directly, but apparently she wants to do it in her husband's memory. She doesn't want all his hard work and love for the town to be forgotten."

"Did you report on the murder?" Stacey asked.

"Page three," Archie said with a smile.

Stacey turned the page and began to read. "Not many official quotes," she said.

"Well spotted, Miss Pepper. It wasn't really the right time last night to begin asking for comments. But it's early days."

As Stacey dealt with the re-stocking and the trickle of customers, Archie asked Lilly who she thought would be the best person to speak to in order to get some proper quotes for his follow-up article.

"I'd dearly like to speak to Felicity Russell, but she's refused to talk to the press until after the funeral."

"What about Lady Defoe? I think she and Felicity must be quite close. It was Lady Defoe who was comforting her last night."

Archie made a note.

"I'll do that. I don't suppose you could put in a good word for me with Mrs Russell, could you, Lilly? You both looked to be getting on well at the fundraiser. Could you ask her if she'd see me?"

"It's true. We discussed a number of things and found we had a lot in common. We exchanged numbers, as a matter of fact. But I'm not comfortable doing that, Archie. She's just lost her husband and her nephew has been charged with his murder. Plus, I thought you said she wasn't meeting with any reporters at the moment?"

"Lilly, I am so sorry. That really was insensitive of me. I don't know what I was thinking. Please, put it down to exhaustion after pulling an all-nighter, right after a bit of a boozy shin-dig. I'm used to getting the jump on my fellow reporter brethren and hoped to do the same this time."

"No matter who you use to get your story?" Lilly said. She was feeling annoyed with Archie for not only putting her in such a position, but for thinking he could use their relationship in such a way. Maybe she was feeling a bit out of sorts as well? She didn't usually take offense like this. Especially with Archie.

"Lilly," he said, taking both her hands. "Please, forgive me. You're absolutely right. I should never have asked you. What can I do to make it up to you? I'm throwing myself at your mercy, Miss Tweed. What do you want me to do? Swallow fire? Walk over hot coals? Decorate your spare room? I'll do it. Just you say the word."

Despite herself, Lilly rolled her eyes, then smiled.

"All right, that's enough, Archie Brown. I'll think of some suitable punishment. But," she said, turning serious. "I'll also see if I can get something from Felicity for you. I've already arranged to see her this afternoon. I never got a chance to say how sorry I was for her loss last night. I'm not promising anything, but I know how much it means to you and if I can help, then I will. However, I refuse to take liberties, Archie. It needs to be on Felicity's terms or not at all. And please don't ever ask me to do anything like this again."

Archie jumped off his seat and threw his arms around her, whispering in her ear. "I won't. I promise. Did anyone ever tell you you're one in a million?"

Lilly nodded into his shoulder.

"You. Frequently. I'm almost beginning to believe you."

"I hope you do, Lilly. I mean every word."

$\mathcal{T}$HE DAVIS'S HOUSE was situated in one of the best areas Plumpton Mallet had to offer, at the foot of the moors. A large detached house, and a well-established garden with the back gate opening onto the moorland track. It was an area Lilly had looked into living herself, but the houses were snapped up before she could even make an appointment to view. Sometimes they were bought before officially going on the market. That's how sought after they were.

She'd cycled home and picked up her car, and now parked it on the road at the front, grabbed the tea gift basket she'd put together before leaving, and walked up the drive to the door. She rang the bell and waited. It wasn't long before Felicity answered, dressed in an elegant, short-sleeved, charcoal grey dress with a string of pearls at her neck.

"Lilly, thank you for coming. Please, come in."

"Felicity, I'm so very sorry for your loss," Lilly said as she stepped over the threshold into a hall decorated in white and lemon, with an antique console table covered in sympathy cards, bouquets of white roses and lilies, and a large cut-glass bowl containing bunches of keys.

Felicity nodded and followed her gaze. "They've been coming all morning," she sighed sadly, looking at the floral arrangements. "Friends and relatives, of course, but a lot from the townspeople. Russell was very much loved here." She smiled and shook her head. "Sorry, come on through to the kitchen and I'll make coffee. Or would you prefer tea?"

"Coffee is fine, thank you."

The large, open-plan kitchen was at the back of the house overlooking a beautiful garden and the moors beyond. Again, it was beautifully appointed, but, as far as Lilly was concerned, rather too modern for her tastes. As well as being incongruous with the age of the house. Then again, she was a fan of vintage.

She laid the gift basket and card on the central white marble island, which doubled as a breakfast bar, and perched herself on a cream leather topped stool while Felicity made coffee using a state-of-the-art professional machine that wouldn't look out of place in the cafe.

"Oh, is that lovely gift basket for me?" Felicity asked, placing a cup and saucer in front of Lilly. "That's very thoughtful. Thank you, Lilly. I'll be sure to make myself a cup this evening to help wind down."

"I read in the paper this morning you're running for mayor in Russell's place."

"Yes, I saw it. I was pleased it was on the front page. It's good PR for my campaign." Lilly hesitated. "You're surprised I'm running so soon?" Felicity asked her intuitively, and Lilly nodded in response.

"I was a little."

"And there are probably others who feel the same way you do. But, by the same token, I also have a lot of support. The fact is, Lilly, I don't want all Russell's hard work to come to nothing. This town meant a great deal to him and he wanted more than anything to see it succeed with new and improved initiatives. I feel the same. There are so many ways in which it can be regenerated and enhanced without spoiling what it is at its core."

She paused to take a sip of coffee, then continued.

"Look, between you and me, Russell was excellent at the meet and greet aspect. Circulating, networking, and, of course, entertaining. But behind the scenes it takes a lot of extremely hard work and organisation. The ideas that Russell was basing his campaign on weren't all his, the majority were Carl's and mine. Russell was glad of my help, but he had outmoded ideas of a woman's place. He felt the job of Mayor was a man's position. He believed it was his right to shine, to be in the spotlight while I supported him from the shadows. It's my turn to shine now, Lilly, and I intend to do just that. For the good of Plumpton Mallet, of course."

Lilly took a sip of the excellent coffee.

"You mentioned Carl. Do you know how he is?"

"Innocent. That's what he is. Russell thought of Carl as his son. There is no way on God's green earth that Carl would murder Russell. He was his role model. The man he looked up to above all others. It's appalling the police have arrested him for such a heinous crime. What motive could he possibly have to kill a man who he considered to be a father? A man who he also worked for. He had a very good position with my husband, Lilly. Not to mention the perks that came with it. A good salary, the car, club memberships, exclusive invitations, elevated social status, and the rest. Why would he jeopardise all of that? It just doesn't make sense. Well, he has the best legal representation possible. I've seen to that. I have every confidence he'll be released soon."

They talked for another hour or so, with Felicity willing to give Lilly a quote for Archie to use with regard to her ideas for the town, but nothing personal, or about the death of Russell. The main one being the synergies she saw between the shops and businesses and what they could do to promote one another's services.

"Your situation is a prime example of exactly what I mean, Lilly. I know you own both The Tea Emporium and The Agony Aunt's cafe, but your cross promotion between the two is an excellent initiative. I want to encourage other business owners to do likewise."

Lilly agreed it was a good idea and on her way back to the shop called Archie with Felicity's quote.

"Thank you, Lilly. I do appreciate it."

"You're welcome. I'm sorry I couldn't get you anything more with regard to Russell, but she was adamant Carl was innocent. She doesn't mind you printing that."

"And what do you think, Lilly?" Archie asked.

"Hang on, let me pull over."

A moment later, she took the phone off hands-free and picked it up.

"I think she might be right, Archie. It just seems too obvious that the murder weapon was found in Carl's car. I assume Bonnie has already told you that little tidbit, and I haven't put my foot in it again?"

Archie laughed. "Don't worry, she told me. Although I'm not to write about it yet on pain of having my fingernails pulled out one by one. But, I agree with you. If someone is trying to frame Carl, and it does look that way, then they made a poor job of it."

"It's obviously the real murderer who planted the knife. But if Carl didn't do it, Archie, then who did?"

"Well, whoever it is, they're either stupid, playing a clever game of double bluff or dislike Carl enough to want see him stew for a while. I wonder if Carl has any enemies?" Archie mused.

"I've no idea. I'm sure Bonnie is on the case, though. As for me, I'm keeping out of it. Right, I need to get back to work. Speak later, Archie."

"Ciao for now."

*A*T THE TEA Emporium, Lilly said goodbye to several customers who, having just been served, were all clinging onto numerous bags while on their way out of the door, and chatting excitedly about their purchases and 'what a darling little shop' it was. She turned to find Stacey staring morosely at her phone.

"Is everything all right?"

Stacey sighed. "I have a big project for college and one of the team just pulled out. I need to get someone else. I'm sorry, Lilly, but can you do without me for the rest of the day?"

"Of course I can, Stacey. College work comes first. We agreed to that at the beginning. If it gets busy, then I've others I can call on for a couple of hours' extra work. You go and sort out your project."

"Brilliant. Thanks."

Half an hour after Stacey had left, the bell above the door rang, and turning, Lilly came face-to-face with a huge bunch of flowers.

"Lilly Tweed?" the deliveryman asked.

"Are they for me?"

"If your name is Lilly Tweed, then yes."

She smiled, almost certain she knew who they were from.

"There's a lovely smell coming from that teapot," the delivery man said. "What is it?"

"Rooibos and Cinnamon. Would you like a cup to take with you?"

"I would. Thanks."

Lilly served it in one of the take away mugs Stacey had designed for the season and handed it over.

"How much do I owe you?"

"It's on the house," Lilly replied. "For bringing me such a gorgeous bouquet."

"They're not from me, you know."

Lilly laughed. "I know that."

Once he'd left, Lilly turned the card which accompanied the flowers. As she'd thought, they were from Archie. She called him.

"They really are beautiful, Archie. Unnecessary, but I love them. Thank you."

"It's an apology for being such a cad and a bounder. I can't think what possessed me. It's also a thank you for speaking to Felicity Davis on my behalf. Now, enough of that. Let me take you out to dinner. You say when and I'll arrange the whole thing. I think a spot of posh nosh is in order. What say you, Miss Tweed?"

Lilly agreed and after a couple more minutes of conversation, she hung up, put the flowers in a vintage jug on the counter and prepared to deal with her customers. But, annoyingly, her conversation with Felicity and the murder wasn't far from her thoughts.

According to the newly bereaved widow, while the relationship and marriage looked perfect from the outside, behind the scenes, it was another story entirely. But would the fact her husband constantly pushed her away from the limelight yet expected her to work for him be enough motive for murder? It was a bit flimsy, but people had killed for less. And what about Carl? It appeared Russell was far closer to Carl than his own wife, and the murder weapon was found in his car. But Lilly couldn't come up with a suitable motive for him. He was doing very well out of his uncle's position. Surely he wouldn't want to risk it all? She wasn't wholly convinced of his guilt, but on the other hand, she wasn't sure he was innocent either. Like Archie had said, it could be a double bluff leaving the knife in the one place the police would be sure to find it. But why take the knife in the first place? Why not just leave it in the body? Unless the whole point was to frame Carl. In which case, it wasn't him who'd killed his uncle.

She sighed. She was just going round in circles. And she'd sworn she was keeping out of it this time.

"Come on, Earl. Time to go home. Let's forget all about this case. Bonnie is more than capable of solving it."

Chapter Eight

"OH, WHO ARE the flowers from?" Stacey exclaimed the next morning. "They're awesome."

"I agree. A beautiful display," James said. He'd decided to stay for a while after the mayoral fundraiser. "And all your favourites, if I'm not mistaken?"

Lilly nodded. "They're from Archie."

Stacey grinned. "Yep. It's definitely love. And maybe an apology, right?"

"Apology?" James asked. "Oh dear. What did the poor man do?"

Lilly waved the question away.

"Nothing too serious. We're fine. He sent them as a thank you for getting a quote from Felicity Davis yesterday."

"And to say sorry," Stacey said, smirking, not prepared to let it lie.

"Yes, all right, smarty pants. It was to apologise, too."

James raised his eyebrows.

"I'll tell you later, dad."

"So how is Felicity?" James asked, pouring them all a calming chamomile tea from the freshly brewed pot.

"Actually, much better than I'd thought she'd be. I was expecting floods of tears and abject grief, but she was really calm and together. In dress as well as emotionally. It was a bit weird now I come to think about it. A bit 'Stepford Wives,' if you know what I mean? Maybe she's in shock and the reality hasn't sunk in yet. I don't know."

"I must say I was surprised to read in the gazette that she was running in her husband's place," James said. "The poor man isn't even in the ground yet and she's already thinking about his job."

"I think most of Plumpton Mallet feel the same way. But she does have a lot of support."

"So, what else did you find out?" Stacey asked.

"Just so we're on the same page, none of this goes any further than the three of us. According to her, Russell deliberately kept her in the background, wanting the limelight for himself. But he wasn't above using her intellect and skills to further his own cause. She seemed a little bitter about it, although put a brave face on."

"That would bug me, too," Stacey said. "I'd expect my husband to support me in the same way I'd support him. Isn't marriage supposed to be about mutual respect and equality?"

Lilly nodded. "Of course. If you're in an equal partnership, then the marriage is more stable. There's less conflict, less dependency and less resentment."

"Have you heard of John Gottman?" James asked, his university professor hat firmly in place. Lilly and Stacey shook their heads.

"He's an American researcher and psychologist. He found that husbands who accepted their wives' influence are four times less likely to divorce or have an unhappy marriage. And he should know. He's been working on divorce prediction and marital stability for over four decades."

"How do you know all this odd stuff, dad?" Stacey asked in amazement.

"I have a good memory. But I also had the privilege of visiting The Gottman Institute many years ago and met the man himself. We got on very well."

Stacey leaned in conspiratorially and whispered. "With all that resentment festering away for years, do you think she killed him and framed Carl?"

"The thought had crossed my mind," Lilly said. "Apparently, her campaign manager advised her against posting Carl's bail because of how it would look. I don't know whether to believe that or not. She told me she thought Carl was absolutely innocent of the crime, but she's not prepared to go against her campaign manager's advice at the moment."

"Well, she would say that, wouldn't she?" Stacey said. "I mean, if she is guilty, then it's better for her to have Carl accused and locked up, right?"

"Well, that's simply awful for Carl if he is innocent. But what about opportunity?" James asked. "Did she have the time to do it at the fundraiser?"

Lilly nodded.

"I think so. We know of a possible motive now, but she also could have an extra set of keys to Carl's car. It was her husband that bought it for him. Which means she could also have planted the knife."

"Gee, I wonder if you're right," Stacey said, biting her lip.

"All the pieces are there," Lilly said. "But what we don't have is proof. Although we could be barking up the wrong tree entirely."

Just then the shop bell tinkled and a flood of tourists entered. They were kept busy for the rest of the day, with only a quick stop for lunch each.

At closing time, Earl followed Stacey and James to the rear door.

"Looks like he's staying with you tonight," Lilly said.

"That's fine," Stacey said, scooping up the cat. "He likes to sit on my knee while I study. See you tomorrow, Lilly."

ﾟﾟﾟﾟﾟ

LILLY LOCKED THE shop door and hurried across the market square. Glancing at the clock, she saw she still had half an hour before the library closed. She'd received a message to say the book she'd wanted was now ready for her to collect.

She jogged up the stone steps and pushed open the door. It was quiet and peaceful inside and smelled of furniture polish, wood and earth with a hint of vanilla. She nodded at the librarian, indicating she'd browse for a while before collecting her book, and then moved toward the history section.

She turned the corner and bumped into someone coming in the opposite direction. It was Mrs Davenport, the town gossip. Although she'd be upset at hearing herself described in such a way.

"Sorry, Mrs Davenport," Lilly whispered.

"Oh, hello, Lilly," the woman whispered back. Although it was nearly closing time and the place was almost empty, they still adhered to the no noise rule of the library. "Don't worry, no harm done. How are you? I must say I was sorry to hear about the death at your last catering event. It must have been a terrible shock?"

"It was. Although it wasn't anything to do with my catering, you know."

"Of course not. I didn't mean that. Have you heard Felicity Davis is running for mayor?"

Lilly nodded. "It was in the paper."

"Absolutely astonishing, isn't it? You'd have thought she'd at least have waited a decent interval before announcing her intention. Her poor husband has just been murdered, for goodness' sake. I really do think it's in terribly poor taste."

She gave Lilly a sideways glance. Lilly remained quiet, but with an interested and what she hoped was an encouraging look on her face. She knew some gossip was forthcoming. And while she wasn't usually one to take notice of this sort of thing, if she was going to get to the bottom of the murder, she needed all the help she could get.

"Of course I'm not terribly surprised," Mrs Davenport continued in an even lower whisper. "It's common knowledge Russell didn't treat her very well."

"Oh?" Lilly said, wondering what else the woman was privy to. She wasn't aware others knew about the difficult relationship between the Councillor and his wife. But, she supposed, those closest to the couple most likely would have picked up on it. Then again, Felicity had been quite happy to tell Lilly about it. She may have told any number of people.

"Oh yes," Mrs Davenport went on, bustling with importance. "Of course, Russell and his sister had that dreadful fight about their inheritance. Did you hear about it?"

"No, I didn't."

"I understand he took the lion's share, which she was not happy about."

Lilly wondered if that was the reason for the snippet of argument she'd overheard between Carl and his uncle at the fundraiser.

"Apparently, his sister also accused him of insulting his own wife at some family get together. A reunion or something, I'm not sure of the details." She waved her hand dismissively as if to say, if I don't know about it, then it's not important. "The only reason Russell hired Carl was to smooth things over with his sister, and we all know how that turned out. No, that boy really isn't bright enough for that sort of job. Not politically savvy by all accounts either. If you ask me," she said, leaning in even further. "His driveway doesn't go all the way to the road."

Lilly looked down while covering her mouth with her hand to hide a smile. She'd not heard that particular expression before. Although she got Mrs Davenport's gist. She was surprised to learn there had been animosity between Russell and his sister. The last she'd from Archie was they got on well. But this new information certainly gave Carl more of a motive for killing his uncle. She wondered if Carl and his mother had been left particularly cash strapped without their inheritance?

"Well, my dear, I really can't stand about chatting like this," Mrs Davenport said, as though it had been Lilly who'd waylaid her and not the other way around. "I must get on. I do hope this dreadful murder doesn't prevent you from getting more catering events. It would be such a shame."

And it would give you something else to gossip about, Lilly thought privately. She said goodbye and went to collect her book. Walking back to the market square, she realised the one person who could shed light on what she'd just learned was Carl himself. At the very least, as her friend and a concerned citizen, she should let Bonnie know about what she'd just learned. Oh, who are you kidding, Lilly Tweed, she admonished herself. You just can't keep away. You're going to snoop no matter what you tell yourself.

She changed direction and began to walk toward the police station.

☙❧

SHE PUSHED OPEN the heavy station door and entered. At the front desk, two women were speaking with the desk sergeant. One was Felicity Russel, the other she didn't recognise. She hesitated, then moved to the notice board. It would give her something to do while she waited to see if Bonnie was available.

"I've already paid his bail and handed over his passport. So when will my nephew be allowed to leave?" Felicity was asking.

Lilly started. Felicity had said she wouldn't be posting bail when she'd visited her. She wondered what had changed mind. A moment later, she got her answer.

"He's being processed now. I need you to sign some paperwork to say you understand he's to reside at your address for the duration. That he is not to speak to anyone connected with the investigation and he needs to report here, to the station, once a week on a day and time, which we will give him. Failure to adhere to these conditions means he may be arrested again and taken into custody."

Felicity nodded. "Yes, I understand."

"My son and I will both be staying with Mrs Russell until this dreadful business is over," the second woman said in a shaky voice. Obviously, this was Carl's mother. Russell Davis's sister. Tall, thin, and in slightly shabby, but well kept clothes that would have been new around five years previously. She looked nothing like either her brother or her son. Her hair, once dark, was now streaked with grey and pinned in a careless chignon. She wore small gold stud ear-rings and no make-up. Her face was grey and strained, making her appear at least ten years older than she probably was, Lilly thought. Felicity Russell, by contrast, was impeccably turned out.

With the paperwork being prepared, both women turned to wait for Carl.

"Oh, Lilly. Hello. What are you doing here?"

"Hello, Felicity. Actually, I just called in on the off-chance to see if Bonnie was free."

"No, she's out, apparently. I naturally asked to see her first, with her being the detective in charge."

"Oh, okay. Sorry, I couldn't help but overhear. You've had a change of heart about posting bail?"

"I have. Despite my campaign manager's protests, I couldn't bear to think of Carl languishing in jail when he's innocent. He's family. Someone is obviously out to put the blame on him and we need to find out who and why. We can do that better when we're all free to put our heads together and talk at home. Sorry, where are my manners? This is Josephine Bates, Carl's mother. Jo, this is Lilly Tweed. She did all the catering for the fundraiser."

The two women shook hands.

"Please accept my condolences for your loss," Lilly said.

"Thank you. Felicity," she said, turning to her sister-in-law. "I can't thank you enough for helping. You know I would have posted bail myself if I'd had the means."

"It's the least I can do. We all know what a shoddy thing Russell did to you both. But would you mind keeping it a secret? My campaign manager is quite correct in that regard. It wouldn't look good if it became common knowledge it was me who was responsible for freeing the supposed murderer of my husband just because he's family."

"Of course I will. My only concern is getting Carl out of jail and safely home."

"Lilly, you don't mind keeping quiet about it, do you?" Felicity asked.

"My lips are sealed," Lilly replied with a smile.

"Mrs. Davis," the sergeant called out. "I have the paperwork ready for your signature."

With Felicity busy at the desk, Lilly took the opportunity to talk with Josephine. Considering the way she'd been treated by her brother, she'd been added to her list of suspects.

"I'm very sorry about all you're going through. It must have been a terrible shock to learn of your brother's death and the fact your son was being blamed?"

"I don't care one way or another about Russell. My priority is my son."

Lilly was a bit shocked at the callous way Josephine spoke about her brother, but did her best not to let it show.

"Were Carl and his uncle close?" she asked, idly wondering what had happened to Carl's father.

"Yes, unfortunately. Carl thought Russell walked on water and applied for the post without my knowing. He was convinced he'd got the job fair and square based on his experience. I knew otherwise, but kept my mouth shut. Russell thought he could win back my affection by hiring my son. The only time Carl spoke ill of my brother was when Russell cheated me out of my inheritance. He knew I was upset, but applied for the position, anyway. There was nothing I could do or say to change his mind. Russell was the sort of person who thought he could buy whatever he wanted. He took Carl everywhere with him. Bought him a car, wined and dined him, took him on expensive trips and introduced him to all the right people. And by that I mean the ones with the money. Carl, in the face of all that wealth, glamour and importance, didn't stand a chance. Although, to his credit, Russell treated him like a son. Which is why

I'm stunned anyone would believe Carl would kill him. It's ludicrous. Someone is trying to frame him."

Felicity joined them a second later and a few minutes after that a very dishevelled and bewildered looking Carl joined them. He looked exhausted, with dark circles under his eyes and a haunted look in his eyes. A far cry from the confident, slightly arrogant, smart young man Lilly had met at the fundraiser. Josephine rushed over.

"Oh, my God, Carl. Are you all right?"

"I'm fine, mum. Tired but I'm okay. I just want to get home."

"And that's where we're going. We'll sort it all out. Don't worry, Carl," Felicity said. She nodded at Lilly and the three of them left.

"Do you need help, Lilly?" The desk sergeant said.

"Actually, I was looking for Bonnie, but Felicity said she was out. Is that right?"

"It is. Back in the morning."

"Okay, thanks."

Outside, there was no sign of Felicity's car. They had obviously whisked Carl away as quickly as possible. Lilly was disappointed not to have been able to speak with him, but she'd also gleaned some interesting and potentially useful information.

*T*HAT NIGHT IN bed, with her feet mercifully free of the weight of Earl Grey, Lilly got a notebook and began to write down what she knew, or could surmise, so far.

Russell Davis had been found dead outside the rear of the premises. A fatal stab wound being the cause of death and, as Bonnie had subsequently discovered, the weapon belonged to a set from the venue's kitchen. Not one of Lilly's or Abigail's thankfully, but by grabbing something near to hand and conveniently available, as opposed to bringing a weapon with them, could mean the murder possibly wasn't premeditated.

Later, in the car-park opposite, when Carl was being interviewed, the knife had been found by Bonnie in his car and he'd been arrested. A plant or a clever double bluff?

Josephine Bates, Russell's sister and Carl's mother had not been at the fundraiser, but she certainly wasn't sorry her brother was dead. And Lilly suddenly remembered Carl saying he'd spoken to her on the phone that same night. Could she have encouraged Carl to kill his uncle in light of the inheritance he'd cheated her out of? They could have been working together from the start. Lilly herself had overheard a tense argument between the two men, and Russell had threatened to withdraw any help for the two of them, whatever that meant, if Carl persisted in asking about whatever it was they'd been discussing.

Then there was Felicity. Again, like her sister-in-law, she didn't appear to be grieving the loss of her husband. She was naturally at the event, so had access to the kitchen and the knife. She could have arranged to meet Russell outside. He wouldn't think twice about meeting his own wife, slipped away and killed him. Then, with the spare keys to Carl's car, which she could have taken at any time considering it was Russell who had bought it, she'd planted the murder weapon and returned to the event with no one the wiser.

But, family aside, there were others who could have wanted the Councillor out of the way. She wrote down Mayor Kenneth Goodwin and sighed. She hated to think he was responsible for the death of his rival. She liked him and he'd worked hard for the town and its residents and businesses alike. But he'd held the post for so long, perhaps he didn't know how to do anything else? Lilly could hardly remember the previous incumbent, Potter or Pritchard, maybe? That's how long Goodwin had been in the post. It could be something as simple as not being prepared to relinquish the title and position he'd held onto for so long, so had decided to literally do away with the competition. She wasn't convinced, but he was undoubtedly a suspect.

Then there was the butcher, Luke Moore, who stood to lose his home and business should Russell Davis be voted in. A business which had been in the family for generations. There'd been two altercations which she'd witnessed, so in all likelihood there had been others as well. Had he waited until the opportunity to get rid of Russell Davis presented itself on the evening of the fundraiser and taken it? Both Goodwin and Moore had motive and opportunity, but with the large number of speakers during the evening, not to mention the crowd of attendees, anyone could have slipped out and killed Russell.

She needed to widen her scope of suspects. But if she did, it would raise a lot more questions. Questions she had no way of knowing the answers to.

She put the notebook and pen on the beside table and turned off the lamp. She was too tired to think about it any more. Perhaps in the light of day she'd come up with a way to move forward. She yawned and turned over. Snuggling comfortably under the duvet, she was asleep within minutes.

Chapter Nine

AS LILLY UNLOCKED the shop door the next morning, she was greeted by a loudly mewling cat who tried to climb up her trouser leg. She quickly scooped him up before his claws did any permanent damage.

"Good grief, Earl. Whatever is the matter? Are you hungry?"

"Don't let him fool you," Stacey said from behind the counter. "He's had two breakfasts already. Dad did bacon for us, and Earl got more than his fair share."

"It was those eyes," James said. "I just couldn't say no."

"Earl Grey, you are incorrigible," Lilly said, laughing. She put him on the floor where he slunk off to his bed, obviously feeling dejected that he'd not managed to pull the wool over his owner's eyes.

"Dad's staying for a while, Lilly. Isn't that great? We've got a few day trips planned."

James smiled. "We have. Frederick mentioned golf."

"I wouldn't have pegged–excuse the pun–you for a golfer, James."

"And you'd be right. I've never played the game in my life. There's a very good course in Plumpton Mallet, apparently. I just hope I don't show myself up. What are you laughing at, Stacey?"

"Fred didn't mean, like, proper golf, dad. There's a crazy golf course just opened in the park. He thought it would be fun for us to try it out."

"Oh, well now, that's much more my thing. Count me in. I must admit, I've been worried I was going to lose my balls in the river."

"Dad!" Stacey said, roaring with laughter.

"What? What have I said now?"

Lilly and Stacey were laughing so hard tears were running down their faces. The fact James was truly oblivious made it even funnier.

"Just stop, dad, I can't breathe."

"I've always wondered," Lilly said, grabbing a tissue from the counter and wiping her eyes. "What they call those little sticks you put a golf ball on?"

"Tee?" James said.

"I'd love a cup."

"Oh, ha ha. Very good," he said to the sound of Stacey's renewed giggling. "I was just about to brew a bilberry or passionflower. How would that suit you?"

"Oh, it arrived! Yes, please, James. I've been looking forward to sampling these. I'll try the passionflower first, I think."

James gave Stacey a withering look. "And what about you, Miss Giggle?"

Stacey grinned. "Yes. Bilberry, for me, please."

"I'm going to work on blending these two," Lilly said. "It's just a case of getting the amounts right. But that will have to wait. It's opening time."

She wasn't expecting a rush today as there were no tourist buses on the schedule, but when she open the door, she found one of the tour guides standing waiting.

"Good morning," he said.

"Gosh, you're early," Lilly said. "Are you working today?" she added, peering over his shoulder, half expecting a crowd of visitors to be in line behind him.

"No, it's my day off today. I've come for some tea and one of the tea sets I saw last time I was in with my group. Honestly, I spend more money than I make on these tours sometimes. Especially here."

Lilly laughed. "I can't say I'm complaining. There's a bilberry or a passionflower blend on the go at the moment if you want to try them?"

"The bilberry sounds good, thanks."

"What tea set were you wanting?"

"That one," he replied, pointing to an art déco style. It was one of Lilly's favourites. A cream base with a dark and light green jungle leaf design and gold plated handles and trim.

"My sister is a collector of all things 1930s and as she's got a big birthday next week. I thought this would be perfect."

While Stacey went to get a boxed set from the store room to gift wrap for him and James poured him a bilberry tea, the tour guide turned to Lilly and told her he'd heard about the death of Russell Davis.

"Must have been awful for you. But from what I've heard, your food and service were excellent, despite the tragedy."

"That's a relief to know. I'll pass the news on to Abigail."

The morning passed quietly, with Archie popping in just before lunch to see how she was and whether she'd learned anything new regarding the murder. It was on the tip of her tongue to let him know Carl had been released, but she'd promised both Felicity and Josephine she'd keep quiet. Bonnie would let him know when the time was right.

After a quick cup of tea, Archie left, and with only a handful of customers during the next hour, Lilly asked if James and Stacey could manage the afternoon between them. There was somewhere she wanted to go.

"Of course we can," Stacey said. "You off sleuthing?"

Lilly grinned. "I might be."

"I thought you were keeping out of it this time?" James said.

"I thought so too. Unfortunately, my brain won't rest until I find out what happened."

"Well, be careful," Stacey said, her features marred with concern. "Don't go getting into trouble."

"I'll try not to. I never do it intentionally, you know."

"I know, but trouble seems to follow you."

"Well, if it makes you feel any better, I'll keep looking over my shoulder just to be on the safe side."

*ILLY EXITED THROUGH the back door and walked across the cobbled lane to the car-park. Under normal circumstances, when the weather was good, as it was today, she'd cycle into work with Earl happy in his carrier in the front basket. Today she'd driven in. Her subconscious must have already known she'd need the car in order to continue the investigation into Russell Davis's death.

She left the car-park and took a right onto the main street. At the top, she turned left. Her destination was Luke Moore's butcher shop on the outskirts of town.

Five minutes later, she parked across the road from the shop and was just getting out of the car when she saw Luke exit. He was looking at the sign he'd just positioned in the window. As she approached, she was shocked to discover it said 'Vote for Davis.'

"Now, that's something I never thought I'd see."

"Oh, hello, Lilly," Luke said, turning.

"Why the sudden change of heart, Luke? The last time I saw you and Russell you were on the verge of a full-blown fight."

The butcher nodded, a sheepish look on his face and his cheeks turning red. "Yes, my anger got the better of me that day, I'm sorry to say. That, and the worry of losing my home and my livelihood. I think I need to pop by your place and get some calming tea. But, actually, this is in support of Mrs Davis. She came round and spoke to all us business owners.

She doesn't believe in the vision her husband had. She wanted to allay our fears and make sure we all knew her plans for developing this area of Plumpton Mallet are vastly different from his. We listened and asked questions and, well, all I can say is she's got my vote."

"And the other shop owners are in agreement?"

"Oh yes. As you can see, they've all put up signs in support. We really believe she can improve the area and our business without knocking everything down, which was her husband's appalling idea."

"Well, that's good news, Luke. I'm really pleased for you."

"Don't get me wrong, I didn't like Russell or his ideas, but I'd never have wished that on him. It was horrible the way he died. But I'm glad Felicity has taken up the mantle."

"I meant to ask you. After your argument with Russell, did you stay on at the event?"

Luke nodded.

"Thankfully, your Archie calmed me down and 'made me see the error of my ways.'" He put the last in air quotes and Lilly knew those were Archie's words he was repeating. "At the time, I was supporting Kenneth Goodwin, and I wanted to stay and support him. But, with Felicity's ideas, I've changed my mind. Goodwin, like his name, has been good for the town and in the main he's left us alone at this end. But, it's time for something new. A fresh approach to bring us into the twenty-first century, and I don't think Ken can do that. He's been in the job so long he's set in his ways. No, we need a modern approach, and I think Felicity Davis is the one to do it."

Lilly wondered if Kenneth Goodwin was aware of what was being said about him, and how successfully Felicity was rounding up what were, once upon a time, his voters.

"So, what can I get you, Lilly?" Luke said, returning inside.

Lilly's intention hadn't been to buy anything, but now she was here, she realised there were some things she wanted. Following him inside, she ordered ham to go with a salad for dinner. Two pork pies, a pound of sausages, and finally some bacon for Stacey and James. The least she could do was replace what her greedy cat had eaten.

She thanked him and came away with her parcel. But her overriding thought was that Luke Moore certainly knew how to wield a knife.

SHE PARKED BACK in town and dropped into the tea shop to put the meat in the fridge. Stacey and James were both busy with customers, so she waved and left them a note to say she was on her way to the Town Hall, but would try to be back before closing. She was hoping she could get in to speak to Kenneth Goodwin.

There were several members of the press congregating outside when Lilly arrived. She didn't recognise any of them. A quick glance at their press lanyards revealed they were from further afield. County and city newspapers. The murder of a Councillor was obviously big news. Unsurprisingly, Archie wasn't among them. As a local, he was well connected and, when she allowed, obtained his information directly from Bonnie, the head of the investigative team. Lilly took the steps to the entrance two at a time and was awarded with nothing more than a cursory glance. They'd obviously identified her as not being part of the council and therefore not important.

Inside she found security had been stepped up in light of what had happened to Russell Davis, and, along with sweeps of a handheld metal detector, handbags were being checked by a guard. Luckily, she recognised the guard currently on duty. He was the son of one of her regular customers.

"Hi, Jason."

"Hello, Lilly. What are you doing here?"

"I was hoping to have a word with the Mayor. Is he available?"

"No can do, Lilly. I'm sorry. Unless you're on the list, I can't let you through. They're taking no chances now, what with Councillor Davis's murder. No one knows if he's the only one targeted, you see."

Lilly nodded. It had never crossed her mind the murder could be connected to the town council as opposed to Russell himself.

"Don't worry, I understand. Thanks anyway. How's your dad, by the way?"

"On his holidays in Cornwall with my sister. He packed enough tea for a month. He swears it's helping his condition."

"I wondered why he bought so much the last time he was in."

"He took his special tea set, too. The plastic one you got for him. Didn't want to break anything while he was there, what with the shakes he's got. But, I think he's improving slightly, which is great. And all thanks to you."

85

Lilly shook her head. "I didn't have much to do with it, Jason. It was your dad who worked out the tea was helping. All I did was get it for him. I'm very glad to hear he's improving. Send him my best when you speak to him next."

"I will. Thanks, Lilly."

Back outside, she found Laurel Flowers had temporarily double parked outside the building and was struggling to lift several boxes from the boot of her car onto a waiting dolly. Not being able to speak with the mayor was disappointing, but Laurel, as his assistant, was the next best thing. Currently, she was surrounded by the reporters, all clamouring for information and a quote, but not one of them offering to help. Laurel was studiously ignoring them. If just one of them had offered their assistance, they might very well have found the favour returned. Lilly shook her head and shoved her way through.

"Can I help, Laurel?"

"Lilly! Oh, my gosh. Yes, please."

The two of them made short work of retrieving the boxes and pushing the laden dolly up the ramp into the foyer.

"Would you mind staying for a minute and keeping an eye on this lot while I go and park the car?" Laurel asked. "The last thing I need is a parking ticket."

"Yes, of course. No problem."

"Thanks, Lilly," Laurel said when she returned. "I'm glad you were here, or I'd still be struggling outside, surrounded by vultures. What are you doing here, by the way?"

"I came to see the mayor, but apparently I need to be on the list to get into see him."

"You do. He's booked solid today. There's no chance of a meeting, I'm afraid."

"Well, maybe I can help you with these, seeing as though I'm here?" Lilly said, indicating the boxes.

Laurel hesitated for a moment, then nodded. "I'm sure it will be fine. We're seriously short-staffed at the moment. I think what happened to Russell has scared people away."

This time Jason, having searched Lilly's bag and waved the wand over her, allowed them both through and Lilly found herself in the part of the Town Hall reserved for staff or visiting dignitaries only. It was stunning inside with marble floors and deep honey coloured panelling on the lower half of the walls. Above there were several paintings of Plumpton Mallet from hundreds of years ago, alongside portraits of the building's financier and the various mayors through the years. At the far end of the row was one of Kenneth Goodwin in all his civic regalia; wearing the chain of office, and with the mace and sword on display behind him. It was probably done during one of his earlier terms, as he looked a lot younger.

Laurel led her down a corridor to a lift, which Lilly was extremely relieved to see. It would have been impossible for the two of them to lug the boxes up the stairs.

Inside the lift, Lilly glanced at Laurel with concern. She looked utterly exhausted. Her normally perfect hair was unkempt and falling out of her bun, and the expertly applied makeup couldn't completely conceal the shadows under her eyes.

"So, where to?" she said, grabbing the dolly as the lift doors opened on the second floor.

"The archive room," Laurel replied. "It's down here."

"What is all this stuff, anyway?" Lilly asked as she carefully maneuvered the trolley down the corridor. Thanking her lucky stars, it was a parquet floor and not carpet. "Or is it confidential?"

"Mmm, the odd bit perhaps, but no, not really. We're in the process of digitising all the old documents from donkeys years ago. You won't believe how far they go back. There are heaps in there written in the finest copperplate you'd ever wish to see. All in old English. The history is amazing. You can track the beginnings and subsequent development of Plumpton Mallet through all the maps, planning permission, architectural drawings and changes of ownership and use of the buildings. As well as the new roads and bridges. It's fascinating, actually."

"It must have taken you ages to go through this lot," Lilly said in awe. Laurel laughed.

"Lilly, this isn't even a tenth of it. We've got volunteers on board for the less sensitive stuff. The library and Tourist Information staff. Myself, obviously, and a number of the council secretaries. It's a massive undertaking."

"Yes, I can see that. But it's such an important job, isn't it? The whole history of the town at our fingertips would be incredible. I bet the historical society is thrilled."

"Oh yes, they're helping too. Although they're a lot slower than the rest of us, as they keep stopping to read and research everything. It's like putting a load of children in a massive sweet shop and asking them to pick one favourite. Right, here we are."

She unlocked a heavy oak door and switched on the light. Lilly followed into a large room which looked more like a library reading room than a council office. Several tables with brass, green shaded reading lights dominated the centre. There was floor to ceiling oak shelving on all walls and some free standing to make private reading or study areas. The room didn't have a window, being in the centre of the building, but a stunning Victorian glass cupola let in plenty of light from above.

"Gosh, this is a gorgeous room."

"I know. It's a favourite of mine. Almost totally unchanged from when it was first built. We can stack the boxes here. I'll file them another time."

"I hope you don't mind me saying, Laurel, but you look exhausted."

Laurel hitched herself onto the nearest desk and nodded.

"I am. Between working on the mayor's reelection and now with Russell Davis's death to deal with, I honestly don't think I've had a decent night's sleep for months. My job is to make it as easy as possible for Ken. He's had such a bad year, and this murder is just one more thing to add to the ever growing pile."

"Oh, I didn't realise. What else has happened?"

"It's not really a secret. I mean, you can't keep news such as this quiet in Plumpton Mallet, can you? I'm afraid his wife has left him. She accused him of having an affair. Absolute rubbish, of course, he'd never cheat on his wife, but she was convinced. It really knocked him for six. It's been a bit of a job trying to get him back on track, actually. At one point, early after it happened, he was talking about retiring. Thankfully, nothing came of that and he's back on board again, wanting to do the best job he can for the town."

Lilly was amazed she'd heard nothing about it at all. Especially considering the gossips she knew, immediately thinking of Mrs Davenport. In hindsight, she'd not even considered the fact that Mayor Goodwin was alone on the night of the fundraiser. Russell and Felicity Davis were there as a team, and the majority of the other guests had their significant others beside them, but the only female Ken Goodwin had had for company was his personal assistant, Laurel.

"I don't know anything about it, Laurel," Lilly said now. "I'm sorry to hear the news. He must be devastated."

"Oh, he is. Like I said, he even briefly considered resigning his position as mayor, but Mrs Goodwin had made up her mind. There was nothing he could do about it. Then, not long after she'd gone, Ken found out he wasn't running unopposed. That came out of the blue and knocked even more stuffing out of him. And to top it all, Russell was killed at his fundraiser. It's just been one dreadful thing after another and Ken's really struggling to keep positive. He has to deal with increasingly intrusive questions from the press, and they are relentless. Not to mention the worry that he could be the next target. I honestly don't know how much more he can take."

"He must be under unbelievable stress."

"Yes. And Carl Bates was making it worse by telephoning all hours, demanding he drop out of the race and leave the way clear for his uncle. That man is a bully. But, of course, that's all immaterial now, I suppose. Anyway, I'm just trying to keep the poor man sane."

"He's lucky to have you, Laurel."

"Thank you, Lilly. He's a good man to work for, though, so I'm lucky as well. He never takes his staff for-granted and knows how much work we all put in. And talking of Kenneth,

I really must go. We have back-to-back meetings. Thanks so much for your help."

"You're welcome."

They moved back out into the hall and Laurel relocked the door.

"I'm sorry you couldn't get in to see him today. Do you want me to put you down for tomorrow instead?"

Lilly shook her head.

"No, don't worry, it wasn't important. I'll try another time."

⸎

*T*HE TOWN HALL clock struck five as Lilly descended the steps. It was later than she thought. She sent a quick text to Stacey saying she'd be back in the morning and walked across the road to the railway station car-park. She had an idea. A quick look round and she found the car she was looking for. A silver BMW belonging to Kenneth Goodwin. She took out one of her business cards and, after scribbling a quick message on the back and lodging it under the windscreen wiper, sauntered to the End of the Line Italian coffee shop a few yards away. She ordered a cappuccino and waited at one of their outdoor tables.

Her conversation with Laurel had revealed some interesting information. The fact Ken's wife had left him, plus the possibility of losing the only job he'd known for many years, was a strong motive. Killing Russell Davis and framing Carl, who'd apparently also been threatening him, would leave the way clear. But could the mayor she knew really be capable of murder? And would she have the courage to ask him? Assuming he turned up, that was.

It was nearly six o'clock, and she was on her second cup of coffee when she finally saw Ken Goodwin exiting the building. Trudging down the steps as though the weight of the world was on his shoulders. He crossed the road to his car. Finding the business card, he immediately glanced in the direction of the cafe. She raised her hand in a wave and after locking his briefcase in the BMW, he strode in her direction. It was interesting to Lilly to note his demeanor changed as soon as he was in the public eye. As though he wore the position of town mayor as a cloak he could throw off and on at will. Very good acting skills were obviously needed for the job, Lilly mused.

After a little polite small talk over a shared cafetiere, Kenneth Goodwin's countenance turned serious.

"Am I right in assuming you're looking independently into Russell's death, Lilly? Naturally, I keep up with news about our town and it's well known you've got a bit of a knack for amateur detective work."

"Snooping, you mean?" Lilly said with a smile. "Actually, I had no intention of getting involved originally. But being present at the time and the fact it's constantly on my mind, I feel compelled to see what I can find out."

"And are you having any luck?"

"I'm just talking to people at the moment, so I've not really found out much."

"Well, I'll save you the job of asking the foremost question on your mind. No, I did not kill Russell Davis. We may have had different ideas as to what was the best for the growth of the town, but we weren't enemies by any stretch of the imagination." He gave her a rueful smile. "Then again, I'm hardly going to admit it if it was me, am I?"

Lilly asked if he wanted more coffee and he shook his head. "Thank you, but no. I'm not sleeping well as it is."

"They stock my teas here. I'll order a pot of chamomile. It's very good for stress relief and calming the mind."

A few minutes later, the tea arrived and Lilly poured.

"Just what I need," Kenneth said. "It's been particularly stressful recently. In fact, the whole year has been fraught with obstacles and very taxing, if I'm honest."

Lilly nodded.

"How do you feel about Felicity running for mayor in place of Russell?" she asked.

"A little surprised she announced it so quickly, but she is perfect for the job. We see eye to eye in a way Russell and I never did. It was a bit of a shock to discover he was running against me. I've been in the job for so long and have watched the town grow from strength to strength during that time. I like to think I've had a hand in making the town what it is today. If that doesn't sound too egotistical? But, perhaps it's time for me to bow out graciously. Hand the job over to someone with fresh eyes and a little more youth and energy on their side. As much as I love the job, it's taken a lot out of me both personally and professionally. Perhaps it's time to retire and take up golf." He sighed deeply. "No doubt you've heard the rumours about my wife leaving?"

"Only very recently," Lilly said. "If it's any consolation, I honestly don't think it's common knowledge. I was sorry to hear about it, though. Do you know why it happened?"

Kenneth Goodwin shook his head sadly. "I'm as confused now as I was when she announced she was leaving. She packed her bags and refused to discuss it. Then she was gone. It was as quick as that. We haven't spoken since. All correspondence has been done through solicitors. It's just dreadful. It's taken the wind out of my sails completely."

"It's no wonder you're thinking about retiring."

"If Russell Davis intended to carry on where I left off, then I might have already done so. But his ideas would have spelled disaster for the town and the residents."

"Like knocking down the row of shops on the outskirts?"

"Precisely. That and other highly unsuitable proposals. Left to his own devices, he would have ruined Plumpton Mallet. It's a small, quaint market town, steeped in history and nestled in beautiful countryside. It's a hit with the tourists, who keep the town afloat, for those very reasons. If he'd have won, Russell would have removed its very soul, and I couldn't have that. That's why I remained and started to campaign for re-election, so he didn't irrevocably ruin my home and all the hard work I've put in over the years. But I'm tired and just want the stress and pressure to be over." He drank the rest of his tea and got up to leave. "I really must be going, Lilly. Thanks for the tea. I'll ask Laurel to get me some from your shop."

"I'll put a box aside for you."

"Thank you. I hope I can rely on your discretion about what we've talked about?"

"Of course."

Lilly was thoughtful as she watched Kenneth Goodwin walk back to his car. He seemed genuinely perplexed as to the reason his wife had left him. But perhaps he didn't want to admit it was because of a supposed affair he'd had. Particularly if it was true. It's not the sort of thing you share with relative strangers. She couldn't fault his love for the town and his genuine desire to ensure the essence of what made Plumpton Mallet what it was, remained. But was his passion more obsession? If that was the case, then he had an excellent motive for getting rid of Councillor Davis. Although it pained her to do so, Lilly mentally moved him up a few notches on her list of suspects.

She then made a phone call. There was someone she needed to talk it all through with.

※

"*I* WAS JUST ABOUT to call you, Miss Tweed," Archie said, bending to give her a quick kiss when they met in the car-park behind the Tea Emporium a few minutes later. "But you beat me to it."

"Oh? Why was that?"

"To see if I could persuade you to have an early dinner with me. They're having an Italian week at our favourite pub."

"Archie, I don't need to be persuaded. Especially when it comes to Italian food. Besides, I need to pick your brains and I think better over good food."

"Ah, you've been detecting, I take it? In that case, I think a good bottle of red to go with the meal will help fortify my nerves during the interrogation."

Lilly laughed and slipped her arm through his. "Come on, it's only a ten-minute walk. I can bring you up to date on the way."

Over a shared Caprese salad starter, Lilly asked Archie how well he had really known Russell Davis.

"You mentioned on the day of the fundraiser when we were setting up that you met up socially sometimes?"

Archie speared a slice of tomato and chewed thoughtfully before answering.

"We certainly knew one another. Although, I wouldn't say well. He was a larger-than-life sort of chap. Very effusive, although he did have a tendency to thrust his views on you and not listen to any counter-arguments. People were drawn to him, though. He was friendly and affable, and well-liked in the main. We did meet up for drinks on occasion, usually a few of us together, not just myself and Russell, and he'd ask about getting some free press about his various initiatives. Not in my remit, but I handed him over to the reporter whose job it was. It's funny now I think about it. He never really talked about his private life. How odd."

"What did you think about him running for mayor, Archie?" Lilly asked.

"Surprised. Definitely. I wasn't aware it was a position he was interested in. He'd never mentioned it in any discussions we'd had. Which, considering his ebullience, was unusual. I doubt he'd have made a good job of it, though."

"Oh? What makes you say that?"

"Several reasons, I suppose. He could be a bit hot-headed. I mean, you saw that at the fundraiser." Lilly nodded, remembering the altercation between Russell and Luke Moore. "He had a bit of reputation in that regard, actually. Secondly, as I said, he believed his views and ideas were the only ones worth considering. There was very little middle-ground or room for

96

negotiation once he had his teeth into a plan. And he didn't like anyone to question or contradict him."

"Anything else?"

"Apparently, he didn't really get along with any of the other council members. His plans for the shops on the outskirts were opposed by almost all of them. Then he had the idea to increase the council tax for shops. Both in the town centre and on the periphery. And increase the car-park fees. All ostensibly to bring money that would be used to invest in the town. That all went down like a lead balloon."

"But those are terrible ideas, Archie," Lilly said. "It's hard enough for some of the shop owners to turn a profit as it is. Increasing the taxes would put some of them out of business altogether. And increasing parking fees is ludicrous. We rely on tourists to keep the place going. How many would stop visiting if it cost too much to park? It would badly affect the tour companies too, who would have to raise their prices to compensate. They'd lose customers and that again would mean no tourists for us."

"You're preaching to the converted, Lilly. I'm on your side."

"Why have I not heard about this before?"

"It was in a closed council meeting. One of our reporters was there, but as the whole thing was blocked almost as soon as Russell tabled it, it wasn't written up. We don't report on vague ideas and stuff that doesn't happen, or the paper would be as thick as a telephone directory, full of rubbish and far too expensive to print. He didn't get any support from the others. They vetoed it immediately, thank goodness. Particularly Kenneth Goodwin. I believe Russell was furious and became quite belligerent and rude to Ken. Accusing him of being a dinosaur and not wanting what was best for the town. It became a bit heated and Laurel intervened. Eventually, she calmed them down. Russell left very soon after that. Humiliated and outraged in equal measure."

"I can't understand why Russell would even throw his hat into the mayoral ring if he had no support from the members of the council."

"You and me both," Archie replied, leaning back as the waiter served their main course. Chicken Sorrentina for Archie and Chicken Piccata with capers and lemon for Lilly.

"Are you close friends with the mayor, Archie?"

"Not really. Out of the two of them, I know his ex-wife, Rose, better."

This was news to Lilly, and she wondered why he'd failed to mention it before. Especially as he knew she was investigating Davis's murder. Then again, she'd kept Carl's release quiet from him.

"Oh? Tell me more, Mr Brown," she said, with a raised eyebrow and a smirk.

Archie chuckled.

"Nothing like that, Miss Tweed. You've no worry on that score. Actually, she's helped me out in the past with a couple of my articles. Introduced me, anonymously of course, to a useful source. We became friends as a result. I also respect the fact she kept mum about the separation from her husband. She could very easily have dragged his name through the mud, but she chose to keep quiet so as not to ruin his reputation. She handled the whole thing with dignity and poise. I admire that about her. Kenneth kept his job, and she moved on."

"You mean she found someone else?" Lilly asked, sipping her wine.

Archie shook his head. "No, nothing like that. I mean, she moved away from Plumpton Mallet. She's settled in Timbleby village and is quite happy, by all accounts."

Lilly nodded. Timbleby was about fifteen miles north of Plumpton Mallet. A quaint place surrounded by countryside, with a main street, half a dozen shops, a tea room, a post office, and one pub. Although it was within a twenty minute drive to a couple of larger towns, it was quiet and far cry from busy Plumpton Mallet. Lilly idly wondered what she was doing to keep herself occupied.

"So, have you worked out whodunit yet?" Archie asked.

"Nowhere near."

"Don't look so glum, Lilly. I have every faith in your detective skills. Now, how about a tiramisu to cheer you up?"

Lilly laughed. "That's just an excuse for you to have one, Archie."

"Well, of course it is. So, do you want one, or are you happy just watching me eat mine?"

"I'll join you, Archie. How can I refuse that romantic offer?"

Chapter Ten

*T*HE FOLLOWING SUNDAY, Lilly decided to take a trip to Timbleby village. She wanted to speak with Kenneth Goodwin's wife. She had no idea if it would have any bearing on the murder case, but every bit of information, no matter how small, helped in an investigation she'd found. Sometimes a tiny, seemingly innocuous comment could lead to the clue which solved the whole thing.

At ten-thirty, after a leisurely breakfast for herself and Earl, who was sprawled out on the back of the settee basking contentedly in the ray of sunshine coming through the window, she left her cottage and began her drive.

Living so close, Lilly knew Timbleby well, although she wasn't able to visit as often as she'd like. She'd been with Archie a couple of times. The first for a long winter walk followed by a picnic and hot drinks while sitting in the car admiring the views from the top of the valley. The second was a quick visit to the pub for lunch, followed by a lovely walk, then tea and cakes at the cafe on their return.

The village boasted a couple of private bed & breakfasts which were well patronised for most of the year. It was a popular stop off or meeting point for cyclists, walkers and climbers. Approximately half a mile outside of the village centre, there was also a campsite. A mix of those who wished to use tents or their own caravans, and static homes for both holiday makers and all year-round residents. All of whom used the village. Lilly had welcomed numerous holiday-makers in both The Tea Emporium and the Agony Aunt's cafe who were staying at the Timbleby camp. The rest of the outlying areas were made up of farms. Both animal and crop.

She left the outskirts of Plumpton Mallet five minutes later and after a couple of miles turned right off the bypass and drove carefully through the quaint stone-built houses of the neighbouring village before leaving the residential area behind and reaching open countryside.

The lanes were narrow in this part of the world, with the roads just wide enough for two cars to pass without damaging one another. But there were handy lay-bys periodically in case something larger needed access. Lilly pulled into one a moment later as a tractor came into view. The farmer gave a jaunty wave to thank her as he noisily trundled closer, and after a similar gesture she studied the scenery where she'd stopped while she waited for him to pass.

It was predominantly fields as far as the horizon, their boundaries either hedging or beautiful dry-stone walls, with the odd patch of woodland. She gasped in delight when through a gap in the hedge she spied a brown hare bound into view. It stopped, motionless, black-tipped ears and long whiskers twitching as is turned a large, bright, brown eye on her car. After a moment, as though suddenly remembering an appointment he was late for, he sprinted across the field and disappeared into a small copse.

Lilly smiled and pulled back out into the road now the tractor had gone. Just under twenty minutes later, she reached Timbleby and parked on the central, cobbled strip. Getting out, she glanced around. Although it was Sunday, the small village was buzzing with people. Dog walkers and hikers, cyclists and day trippers, all milling about the shops or stopping for lunch in the pub or the tea room.

With no idea where Rose Goodwin lived, she decided to start at the cafe. The village was small, therefore if it was anything like her own home town, it was likely someone would know where she could be found. And the cafe was one of the main hubs of village life. As if in agreement with this decision, her stomach gave a loud rumble.

The cafe was at the top of the street, with its two low bay windows facing down to the road running perpendicular at bottom and the fields and trees at the other side of the low stone wall. The window displays consisted of old-fashioned kitchen implements, like meat grinders, weighing scales, and a hand-held whisk, all of which would have been familiar sights in many houses in years gone by. There was also a set of blue and white striped Staffordshire Chef Ware in excellent condition. There were vintage cook books stacked on an old suitcase and some wonderful jelly moulds in fantastic shapes. It was all vintage and made Lilly feel right at home.

She pushed open the door and entered.

"*H*ELLO," SAID THE cheery, plump woman behind the counter, who Lilly knew to be the owner. "Welcome to the cottage tea room. Have a seat and I'll be with you shortly."

"Thank you," Lilly replied, moving to the rear, where a small vacant table was tucked into the alcove next to the chimney breast. It was home to a wood-burning stove, now unlit, but Lilly remembered it burning brightly and giving off much needed heat when she and Archie had been the last time.

The tea room was aptly named. It had a stone flagged floor, exposed stone walls and light oak, original beams. Floral cushions on the chairs, crisp white table-cloths, vases of flowers, and the watercolours of local scenes displayed on the walls made you feel as though you were entering someone's home rather than a place of business. It was comfortable and inviting and apart from the one opposite hers, all the seats were taken. It was a popular spot.

She picked up the menu and, after a quick glance, made her choice.

"Now then, what can I get you, dear?" the owner asked, materialising at Lilly's shoulder with an order pad in hand.

"The plowman's and a pot of Earl Grey, please."

"Right you are," she nodded, scribbling furiously. "Are you here on holiday?"

Lilly shook her head. "Actually, I'm from Plumpton Mallet. I'm looking for someone; Rose Goodwin. Do you know her?"

"Oh, you're a friend of our Rose, are you?" Lilly didn't put her right. "As it happens, she comes in for a packed lunch every Sunday to take on her walk." She glanced at the grandfather clock in the corner. "She should be here in about ten minutes. Right, I'll get your lunch."

Lilly couldn't believe her luck. The first place she'd tried, and she'd already found the woman she was looking for. Perhaps she could persuade Rose to fore-go her walk and join her for lunch instead.

Quarter of an hour later, just as Lilly had finished pouring her second cup of tea and was now buttering a warm, crispy bread roll, the door opened and the owner welcomed Rose Goodwin by name. She approached the counter and the two women spoke briefly, casting a quick glance at Lilly, who returned their looks with a pleasant smile.

Rose approached. "I'm Rose Goodwin. I understand you're looking for me?"

"Yes," Lilly said rising. "I'm..."

"Lilly Tweed," the woman replied.

"Oh. Yes. That's right. How did you know?"

"I'll give you three guesses," Rose replied with an amused expression. She took off her coat and, after hanging it on the back of the chair opposite Lilly, sat down.

Lilly chuckled. "Archie rang you?"

"He did. Although I didn't expect you to turn up so quickly."

"I didn't even tell him I was coming."

"Well, he obviously knows you very well. How did you find me?"

"I didn't, really. It was just a guess that someone in the village would know who you were, and as the only tea shop, this seemed to be an obvious place to start."

"I see. All right, I'm happy to answer your questions, Lilly, providing none of it goes any further. Let's wait for my lunch, then I'll tell you what I can."

"I ASSUME YOU'VE HEARD what happened to Russell Davis?" Lilly asked as they continued their meal.

"Yes. A friend from Plumpton Mallet called me the day after the fundraiser. Such a dreadful shock. I couldn't believe it when I heard. Do the police know who did it?"

Lilly shook her head. "No, not yet."

"And Archie said you were there catering the event."

"That's the reason I'm involved. In an unofficial capacity, of course. I just can't seem to stop thinking about it, and rather than put up with constantly disturbed nights, I'm trying to put my mind at rest, as well as gather information for Bonnie. She's a good friend of mine and the detective heading the investigation."

"Yes, I know Bonnie. Not well, but she had dealings with Ken occasionally with regard to the crime prevention initiatives in the town. She always struck me as very efficient and capable. I liked her."

Lilly took a bite of her food to give her time to think. She had a particularly sensitive question to ask and was wondering what the best approach would be. But there really wasn't a tactful way to ask. Finally, she decided to just be direct and get it over with.

"Rose," Lilly said, taking a deep breath. "I hope you don't think I'm being nosy. And please, don't feel you have to answer. But do you mind me asking why you and your husband have separated?"

Lilly could see the pain in Rose's expression as she looked up.

"I wondered when you'd get around to asking that question. The truth is, I discovered my husband was having an affair. I found women's underwear in his overnight bag when he returned from London. A ghastly pink and black lace thong. Very common looking. I would have thought if he was going to have an affair, he could have at least chosen someone with a bit of class, rather than a common hussy. But," she shrugged. "Perhaps that was the appeal. I had absolutely no idea up until that point, and... well, the details don't matter. I can't see it being pertinent to Russell Davis's death."

"I'm sorry," Lilly replied, not knowing what else to say.

Rose nodded. "Thank you. But, infidelity aside, and I'm putting that down to a mid-life crisis, Ken is a good man, Lilly, and passionate almost to the point of obsession about not spoiling Plumpton Mallet. I know your next question will be 'do I think he killed Russell?' and I can tell you, quite categorically, that no, he didn't. He absolutely could not take the life of another human being. He's just not that kind of man. He is gentle and kind. A humanitarian."

Lilly nodded and wondered if Rose realised she had just confirmed the perfect motive for Ken to do away with his rival. It was interesting she'd also used the word obsession. Lilly had thought the same thing herself.

"What was his reaction when you confronted him about the affair?"

"Actually, I didn't."

"What?" Lilly blurted out before she could stop herself. She felt the heat rise in her cheeks. "I'm so sorry. I didn't mean to be so blunt."

Rose nodded. "I know it's not the way most people would address such a life-changing issue as an affair, but let me explain. I left the underwear in an obvious place and waited for him to bring it up. Apologise. But he never said a word. It was a rather passive-aggressive approach, I'll admit, but I did it that way deliberately. I hate confrontation and just couldn't bring myself to speak about it first. I didn't want to talk about the 'other woman.' I didn't want to know anything about her at all. But, to be perfectly frank, the incident gave me the final push I needed to leave. Ken is a workaholic, Lilly, and with our two boys making their own way in the world, I realised we hadn't spent quality time together for a long time. There'd been cracks appearing in our marriage for a good while, and there's only so many times you can paper over them before it's no longer possible. It was better that I left before the apathy turned to animosity and we began to resent one another." She sighed and took the last mouthful of her sandwich before leaning back. "That's really all I can tell you."

"Thank you for speaking with me, Rose, and for being so candid. I know it can't have been easy."

"You have Archie to thank for that," the woman replied, rising and retrieving her coat. "He thinks the world of you. You have a good man there, Lilly, and from what I've seen so far, he has a good woman in you."

They said goodbye and Lilly watched Rose leave, deep in thought. While the conversation hadn't been deeply revelatory, a couple of things had hit Lilly immediately. The first being that Kenneth Goodwin had lied to her.

❦

"*Y*OU DIDN'T MIND me calling Rose and letting her know to expect you, did you?" Archie said that night when he phoned her.

"No, of course not. I'm grateful you did. I don't think she'd have spoken to me if you hadn't paved the way. But how did you know I'd go?"

"It was the look on your face when I told you about her. You didn't need to say anything, your expression was enough. That, and the loud grind of the cogs whirring in your brain."

Lilly laughed. "Crikey, I obviously need to work on my poker-face if I'm that obvious."

"It's only because I know you so well. Once you've got the bit between your teeth, there's no stopping you. I doubt the suspects will notice when you're grilling them, though, so no need to worry. So, did Rose say anything that might help?"

"She caught the mayor out in a possible lie."

"She did? How?" Archie asked, concern in his voice.

"She left because she thought he was having an affair. Apparently, she found some tacky underwear in his luggage when he returned from a trip. She left it in an obvious place in the hope he'd bring the subject up, but he never did. Just carried on as though everything was normal. But when I questioned him, he said he had no idea why she left. It was a complete surprise to him."

"Mmm. I find the thought of him having an affair a bit difficult to believe, to be honest. He and Rose always seemed so happy and well suited. He doesn't seem the type at all. But, then again, what is the type? Look at Charles Dickens, for example. A virtuous life to all outward appearances, yet a sordid affair going on behind the scenes. Well, Ken's either lying and failed to mention the affair to you because he feels embarrassed and guilty. Or, he's telling the truth and is completely innocent. In which case..." Archie stopped talking.

"Archie? Are you there?" Lilly asked, still smiling at Archie's depth of arcane knowledge.

"Sorry, yes. I was just thinking. If he is innocent, then how was the underwear found on his person? Ha! In a manner of speaking."

Lilly chuckled. "That's conjured up some images I never want to see in reality. Thank you, Archie Brown. But you're right. I'll have a think about that. I may need to speak to Ken again."

"Do you want to talk it all through? See if we can put a few things in order?"

"Haven't you got better things to be getting on with, Archie?"

"Better than talking to you? No, of course not. What a silly question. So, what are your thoughts so far?"

Lilly smiled, feeling a warm glow rise swiftly from her feet and settle on her cheeks. She snuggled into the sofa, Earl asleep on his back next to her, one paw thrown over his face and showing the little white patch on his tummy, and thought about Archie's question.

"Setting aside the Goodwin's for the moment, there's Felicity Russell. She has benefited from her husband's death the most, hasn't she? When I spoke with her, she honestly didn't seem as though she was grieving. And her announcement about running for mayor in his place happened so fast. Literally the day after he'd died! I thought that was very odd and quite tactless. Almost as if that was the plan from the beginning."

"Then again," Archie said, playing his role as devil's advocate. "That could be interpreted as not wanting to waste all the effort her husband had gone to for the town and his campaign. The printing of the literature alone can be jolly expensive, you know."

"I'm not so sure about that. Her ideas are very different from his. She disagreed with what he was planning with the row of shops on the outskirts. She's visited them all and told them of her plans and they've now promised her their votes. Although I'll concede you're right about the literature expense. It's her name as well as his, but taking that out of the equation, she's now in the limelight, which is what she wanted. And has wasted no time in getting out there and pounding the pavement looking for supporters."

"Okay, she needs to stay on the list. So who's next?"

"We can't discount Carl yet. The knife was found in his car, but perhaps he put it there to throw Bonnie off the scent?"

"I'm not sure he's clever enough for that, Lilly. But say he did. What's his motive?"

"I don't know yet, but Russell and him were having a bit of an argument on the night of the fundraiser. Russell threatened to stop helping Carl and his mother if he continued to pester him. Whatever that was about could be the reason."

"So, Russell's sister is also on your suspect list?"

"She has to be, I suppose. Although she wasn't officially in Plumpton Mallet when her brother was killed. She only came when she found out Carl had been arrested. But they could have been working together. I met her at the police station and it struck me that she was glad Russell was gone. There was an inheritance they were both due to get, but Russell ended up with it somehow, leaving his sister and Carl quite hard-up according to her."

"Blimey. What a family. I had no idea. So, who else are you thinking about?" Lilly could hear him turn a page in his notebook. Archie tended to make notes during their brainstorming sessions and they'd proved invaluable in the past.

"Luke Moore. He had everything to lose if Russell became mayor. He'd also argued and threatened him in public on numerous occasions."

"He's also an expert with a knife."

"I thought that, too. I think that's everyone."

"The funeral is tomorrow morning at eleven. I'll pick you up at your house half an hour before. Perhaps we'll learn something there."

"Thanks, Archie. Yes, I'm hoping to have a word with Carl if I can. I've not been able to talk to him at all yet."

"All right, Sherlock, I'll be here if you need me."

"Thank you, Watson. See you tomorrow."

Chapter Eleven

ARCHIE PICKED HER up at half-past ten the
following morning, dressed as conservatively
as she had ever seen him, in a three-piece
charcoal herringbone suit and a black tie with fine grey stripes.
Lilly had chosen a knee-length, long-sleeved black dress to
go with her modest heels, and topped it with a long dark
grey coat.

She'd left Earl safely at home in the cottage and Stacey
had messaged her to say she would be able to cope at the
shop for the day.

The service would be in the grade II listed parish church
in town, followed by an internment at the cemetery on the
outskirts. Archie parked on a nearby side road and they walked
up Church Street hand-in-hand. In front they saw other
mourners had done the same and followed them through
the gate and up the stone steps to the entrance.

The church had been built on the site of a roman fort, the earliest part being the 13th century south doorway, which they were now entering. It was distinctly chilly inside, as it was stone tiled and built from exposed stone in a Tudor-Gothic style. Lilly was glad she'd worn her wool coat.

Not being part of the family, and with Archie being more of an acquaintance than a friend, they'd decided beforehand to sit in the rearmost pew. It would also give them both the chance to observe the attendees.

"Golly, these cushions are like bricks," Archie whispered, fidgeting in an attempt to get comfortable. "I hope the service doesn't go on too long or I'm going to lose all feeling from the waist down. You'll have to pick me up off the floor when it's time to leave."

Lilly smothered a giggle. It wasn't an appropriate time or place to start laughing. But she agreed with him. The burgundy velvet pew cushions had been in place for so long, and had accommodated the rears of so many parishioners over the years, that the stuffing was either non-existent or had set like cement. She was feeling the onset of pins and needles herself.

"I don't think I'll be able to, Archie," she whispered back. "I'll be in a heap on the floor with you."

Archie snorted, causing a severe-looking woman in front to turn round and give him a withering stare. Archie mouthed an apology, then grinned at Lilly once the woman had turned back.

The church was filling rapidly, which surprised Lilly a little considering how unpopular Russell Davis was purported to be. The family, who were sitting in the front right pew, consisted of Felicity Davis and Josephine Bates. Immediately behind were Russell's work colleagues and other members of the council, with their significant others. Mayor Goodwin and Laurel Flowers were seated across the aisle with other prominent town residents, including Lady Defoe and her husband. Lilly wondered where Carl was. She got her answer several minutes later as through the arched door came the coffin procession, accompanied by a solemn classical piece played on the church organ. At the front, shouldering the heavy casket, was Carl. He was one of the pall bearers. Atop the coffin were three floral displays in traditional white roses and lilies.

The congregation was still as they made their way down the aisle and placed the coffin on the stand at the front. Carl bowed his head for a moment, then joined his mother and aunt. The other men did likewise and shortly after a white smocked vicar climbed the steps of the square wooden pulpit, and opening the bible began. Lilly felt Archie take her hand and squeeze it. She squeezed back, grateful for the contact. It was at times like these you were inevitably reminded of your own mortality.

*I*T WAS A quiet and respectful procession who followed the coffin and the family out of the church forty-five minutes later, and shook the hand of the vicar, thanking him for the service. Lilly spied Bonnie standing at the back with a colleague and the detective gave her a nod and a brief smile before slipping out into the crowd.

Lilly and Archie made their way back to the car slowly. They didn't want to arrive at the cemetery before the family.

"Was Russell a golfer, then?" Lilly asked, as Archie, waved out by a bus driver, turned right onto church street and joined the flow of vehicles slowly moving toward the traffic lights. On green, he drove over the crossroads and carried on along the main road, turning left a few minutes later.

"Yes. A good one too, by all accounts. He's been a member of the club for a long time, so it's not unusual the wake is being held there."

Lilly realised many of the attendees most probably had been fellow members. Quite a few of the men had been wearing the same royal blue tie with a muted gold emblem beneath their sombre suits.

Archie parked on the road behind several other cars and they walked the short distance to the large black iron gates of the town's only cemetery. With no idea where the plot was situated, they simply fell into line behind the other mourners.

"Is there someone covering for the paper?" Lilly asked quietly as they approached the graveside.

"One of the junior reporters. You probably didn't notice, but she was at the back of the church. She won't be here, though."

Archie grasped Lilly's hand as they took their places at the back of the crowd. Once everyone was in place, the vicar began with John 11.25,26.

"I am the resurrection and the life, saith the Lord: he that believeth in me, though he were dead, yet shall he live: and whosoever liveth and believeth in me shall never die."

As the casket containing Russell Davis' body was made ready to be laid into the earth, the vicar continued.

"Man, that is born of a woman hath but a short time to live, and is full of misery. He cometh up, and is cut down, like a flower; he fleeth as it were a shadow, and never continueth in one stay.

"In the midst of life we are death: of whom may we seek for succour, but of thee, O Lord, who for our sins art justly displeased?

"Yet, O Lord most holy, O Lord most mighty, O holy and most merciful Saviour, deliver us not into the bitter pains of eternal death.

"Thou knowest, Lord, the secrets of our hearts; shut not thy merciful ears to our prayer; but spare us, Lord most holy, O God most mighty, O holy and merciful savior, thou most worthy Judge eternal, suffer us not, at our last hour, for any pains of death, to fall from thee."

Lilly glanced at the family. Josephine was staring resolutely ahead, her face a mask, making it difficult to know what she was thinking or feeling. By contrast, Carl was sniffing occasionally and dashing the odd tear from his cheeks. Felicity looked pained and grieving, but she appeared to be resolutely holding it together and there were no tears.

As the casket was lowered and the handfuls of earth from the family was cast upon the body, the vicar finished with...

"We commend unto thy hands of mercy, most merciful Father, the soul of this our brother departed, and we commit his body to the ground, earth to earth, ashes to ashes, dust to dust, And we beseech thine infinite goodness to give us grace to live in thy fear and love and to die in thy favour, that when judgement shall come which thou has committed to thy well-beloved Son, both this our brother and we may be found acceptable in thy sight. Grant this, O merciful Father, for the sake of Jesus Christ, our only Savior, Mediator, and Advocate."

The group then finished with a collective delivery of The Lord's Prayer and Lilly silently breathed a sigh of relief.

"Strange nobody stood and said a few words about Russell, don't you think?" Archie said once they were back in the car. "Are you all right, Lilly?"

"I think so. I've never been to a burial before. I didn't know what to expect."

"And?"

"I found it archaic and depressing, if I'm honest."

"Yes, it was a bit full on, wasn't it?"

"All that being 'full of misery' and 'being cut down like a flower.' As well as living in fear and being continually judged. I may be getting the whole meaning wrong, but I'd prefer my life to be celebrated for what it was rather than be judged inadequate from the moment I was born. I don't want people to mourn my death, Archie. I want them to celebrate a life well-lived and the things I've achieved to make the world a better place, no matter how small my achievements are, knowing I've gone on to another place to continue the next chapter. Not somewhere better than here, necessarily. I mean this is supposed to be 'Heaven on earth,' if the prayer is to be believed. But, how is being judged and found wanting, and living in fear of retribution when you die for the slightest error or mistake, make you genuinely live better? People who live in constant fear don't live, they exist. How can they see the beauty around them when they're just waiting to die, having done nothing worthwhile in case it was deemed a sin?"

"Good grief!" Archie said, staring at her in astonishment. "It really did get to you, didn't it? You're a positive ray of sunshine, Miss Tweed. Hang on while I get the soap box out of the boot."

Lilly laughed softly, feeling instantly better. "Thanks, Archie."

"I'm not the best person to discuss theology with, Lilly. If you want some answers, you'd be better talking to the vicar. I'm sure he'll put you right. But I do understand what you're saying. It was a bit Victorian, but it's been done like this for aeons. I suppose it boils down to living the best life you can, while helping but not harming others. I've also made a mental note that should I still be around when you move on to the next phase, there will be a big knees up. You can do the same for me. Right, we're here. Let's dust off our melancholy and see if we can shed a bit more light on your case."

ARCHIE PARKED IN the visitor's car park and they followed a group of people already walking to the front of the building. Up several stone steps, beneath an arch where a deep pink clematis was growing, they entered the 19th hole from the wide, stone-flagged terrace, which had magnificent views over the eighteenth hole and the moorland beyond.

Just inside, Felicity greeted them.

"Hello, Lilly, Archie. Thank you for coming."

"It was a beautiful service," Lilly said. "How are you holding up?"

"Providing I keep the proverbial British stiff upper lip and don't think about the reason I'm here too much, I'll be fine. Although I will be relieved when it's all over."

"Yes. I imagine it's exhausting putting on a brave face continually. Let me know if there's anything I can do."

"Thank you, Lilly. There's a buffet set out in the dining room and the club staff will see to your drinks. Please, do go through."

They'd hardly had time to move into the room, when an efficient waiter bearing a silver tray was at their side inquiring about drinks. Lilly opted for a cup of chamomile tea and Archie a pint of bitter. Within moments, he was back and served them before moving onto the next guest.

"It looks like Balmoral in here, Archie," Lilly whispered, taking in the plush and extremely tasteful beige, grey and royal blue tartan carpet. Through an open door into a private lounge she glimpsed wingback chairs in cream and burgundy tartan, set before a very old arched fireplace in cream stone. Where they stood were grey sofas and occasional tables. And on the walls were watercolours of the town through the ages. The curtains and pelmet adorning the very large bay window she recognised as a William Morris print, and there were matching cushions on the grey upholstered window seat. It reeked of old money.

"It's the oldest club in the county," Archie told her, as they moved to the window seat. "A lot of the professional golfers we have today started out here. There's a waiting list of years to become a member and you need a good bit of money to be able to afford the fees."

He leant forward and mentioned an eye watering figure.

"That's for a lifetime membership?"

"Afraid not. That's annually."

Lilly was flabbergasted. It seemed an extortionate amount of money in order to knock a little white ball across various lawns in the hope of sinking it into a hole. But she supposed much of the appeal came from the social side and the useful networking it would provide.

"Not tempted to become a member, Archie?"

He shrugged.

"I can't see the appeal. I'll watch a local game of cricket if pushed, but I'm not much of a sportsman, to be honest. I'd rather have my head in a good book. Actually, that's mostly what I do when I'm at the cricket anyway, come to think of it."

After they'd finished their drinks, and the cup and glass were whisked away by an ever attentive waiter, they moved to the buffet, filled their plates and decided they'd better mingle.

Lilly spent some time speaking with Lady Defoe, then moved on to some women members she recognised as customers. Archie was weaving his way through the men, stopping to chat and share anecdotes. Very much at ease.

Having laid her empty plate on a nearby table, she stopped a passing waitress to ask where the ladies' room was.

"Through the door at the far side of the ladies' lounge, madam," she replied, gesturing to the open door Lilly had peeked through on arrival.

Inside she saw Felicity had positioned herself in an armchair beside the unlit fire, and was holding court with some of the lady members. She had an untouched glass of orange juice at her side. In the opposite chair, Josephine looked out of her depth. Munching delicately on a plate of food and taking periodic sips from a large glass of white wine. Her all black ensemble exacerbated her ghostly, pallid look.

The powder room was as plush as the rest of the club. White panelled walls, gilded mirrors and bronze wall lights. A vast array of designer soaps and hand creams, displays of fresh flowers in tall vases, and various richly upholstered chairs made it seem more like the snug of a stately home. The small frosted window which, if Lilly had her bearings right, faced the far end of the terrace outside, was open at the top, letting in a pleasant breeze. She was just drying her hands on a freshly laundered white hand towel bearing the club's monogram, when she heard raised voices coming from outside. She moved to the window in order to hear better.

❦

"I DON'T KNOW HOW you have the gall to show your face here, Carl. You should leave."

"What? No, I'm not leaving. It's my uncle's wake. I have a right to be here. More than you do, actually. Why should I leave?"

"Because you killed him, that's why. Everybody knows the knife was found in your car. You're a murderer."

"I am not! I did not kill my uncle. You don't know what you're talking about! The knife was planted in my car to make me look guilty. How do you know about that?"

"It was in the paper, everyone knows. You're nothing but a bully. A nasty, ignorant little boy in a man's suit who thinks he's better than everyone else. You know nothing about how to do your job. You're only in that position because Russell was your uncle and felt sorry for you. Well, I have news for you, Carl. You're not better than everyone else. Far from it. You deserve to go to prison for a long time for what you've done. You make me sick."

Lilly had heard enough. She rushed out through the ladies' lounge, back into the dining room and exited the building. She could see Carl at the far end of the terrace, back up against the wall while Laurel Flowers spat out her accusations. Taking a deep breath, she walked over.

"Is everything all right here?"

Laurel spun round, the look of anger on her face disappearing in an instant. She stepped back and faced Lilly.

"Of course, Carl and I were just having a chat, that's all." She glanced back at Carl, daring him to contradict her. He didn't care.

"No, it's not all right. Laurel just accused me of killing my uncle."

"Is that true, Laurel?"

"Yes, it is actually. Everybody knows he did it. The police arrested him, didn't they? Why he's been allowed to go free, beggars belief."

"Carl is innocent until proved guilty, Laurel," Lilly said. "That's how the law works. If the police have seen fit to release him, then it's because they don't have enough evidence to charge him. You can't go around accusing people of murder without having the facts to back it up, Laurel."

"Oh, it's obvious he did it, Lilly. It's just a matter of time before the police realise it, too. I shall certainly be having a word with them about letting a murderer walk free around

our town and putting innocent people in danger." Laurel
said and stalked back inside.

"Thank you," Carl said, slumping in a nearby chair.

"Are you all right?"

"Not really. Is it true? Does everyone think I killed him?"

"I haven't heard anything," Lilly said truthfully.

"I didn't do it, you know. You do believe me, don't you? I
could never have killed Uncle Russell. Or anyone else. I can't
believe Laurel turned on me like that. I thought we were friends.
I did her a big favour and gave her a lift home the other day.
Her car broke down not far from our house. Well, that's the last
time I'll help her out." He sighed deeply and got up. "I hope
the police find out who really did it, and soon. I'm obviously
the town pariah right now. I want my name cleared so I can
put all this behind me and get on with my life. Look, I better
go in and see how my mother is. She doesn't know anyone
except Felicity, and she's feeling a bit lost."

"I'll come in with you," Lilly said. She wanted to
find Laurel.

കൈലിള

*L*ILLY, AFTER WALKING through the various rooms in search of her, found Laurel in
the powder room. She went to the sink and
washed her hands, giving another woman the chance to
leave before speaking.

"Laurel, what on earth were you thinking having a go
at Carl like that? A wake isn't the place to start pointing
accusatory fingers at anyone, let alone the deceased family."

"I know, I know," Laurel said, holding up her hands placatingly. "But, I don't like the idea of a... possible murderer walking around Plumpton Mallet free, Lilly. It's frightening for everyone. I probably shouldn't have approached him here, I'll admit that, but I'm under so much stress at the moment with Kenneth's campaign, dealing with the press and trying to keep the staff from worrying whether someone else is going to be murdered. They're traumatised about Russell's death and, quite frankly, wondering if one of them will be next. Not to mention my worry about Kenneth himself. He was doing too much to start with. Now it's the opposite. He seems to be having second thoughts about running at all. He's talking about retiring again, which is ludicrous. He's the best man for the job. I really want him to win, Lilly."

"I can see that, Laurel, but you need to have some time for yourself. You'll be no good to anyone if you're worn out and not thinking straight."

"I know. I promise, once Mayor Goodwin wins, I'll take a holiday. But until then, I need to think ten steps ahead, so it all goes smoothly. Right, if you don't mind, I think I need a glass of wine."

Lilly watched Laurel leave and thought a glass of wine sounded like a good idea. She went to find Archie.

Chapter Twelve

THE NEXT MORNING Lilly and Stacey were rushed off their feet with a couple of tour groups coming through, their regular customers popping in to top up on their favourite teas, and several new customers wandering in to browse or purchase tea sets, as well as the new four tier cake stands Stacey had displayed in the window the day before.

Just after eleven o'clock, as things quietened down, one of the locals entered limping quite badly. Lilly dashed round the counter and pulled out one of the stools.

"Good heavens, Claire, what happened?" Lilly asked, helping her to sit down.

"It's arthritis in my hip. A flare-up. Don't worry, I haven't had a fall or anything. I'm on various painkillers and anti-inflamatories, but I wondered if you had anything that might help? I don't want to become reliant on pharmaceuticals if I can help it."

"Actually, I've just taken delivery of some Holy Basil which should help."

"What a great name. I could do with some divine intervention," Claire said, smiling.

"It's a sacred herb in India. They even worship it in specially built shrines," Lilly said, opening a drawer in her apothecary cabinet and removing a package. "They also use it as a herb to add flavour to their food. It comes from the mint family."

"How interesting," Claire said, leaning forward to smell the leaves. "So, how do I brew it, Lilly?"

"Just steep one teaspoon in a cup of boiling water for about four to six minutes. Because of your particular health issue, I'd also suggest cutting up some ginger root and adding that in. It has some excellent anti-inflammatory properties too, and will give a boost to both you and the tea. Just don't use too much, as it's quite strong."

"Do you have the ginger here?"

"I do. Let me get you some."

The root was kept in the fridge in the back storeroom and she'd only taken a couple of steps when she was overtaken by a grey blur. She found Earl sitting and staring at the fridge door. He gave a plaintive mewl when she joined him.

"Earl, I realise your food is in the fridge, but you can't possibly be hungry. You've had two breakfasts already."

Earl continued to stare at her, his eyes getting bigger and bigger. That was the thing with cats. They knew how to tug at your heartstrings. And she was aware Earl would leave food in his dish if he was full, so he really must have hunger pangs. She scruffed his ears.

"Oh, all right, you win, Mr Grey."

She filled his dish and left him to eat while she returned with the ginger for Claire. She was sipping on a cup of Holy Basil that Stacey had made for her.

"Do you like cherries?" she asked, as she bagged up the order.

"Yes. Why?"

"The tart cherries have even higher antioxidant levels than blueberries and have powerful anti-inflammatory properties. If you eat twenty cherries, or the equivalent in juice concentrate a day, according to the American Chemical Society they could provide the same pain relief as aspirin or ibuprofen."

"Really? Well, that's good to know. I'm on my way to the supermarket next. I'll add them to my list. Thank you so much, Lilly."

"You're welcome, Claire. Just one other thing," she said, helping Claire off the stool and handing over her bags. "Some teas can interact with medicine, so please talk to your doctor just to make sure you're okay to drink them."

"I have an appointment at the clinic in the morning, so I'll ask then. Thanks again."

After Claire had left, Stacey dashed down to the cafe to pick up their lunch from Abigail. She returned with two containers of home made carrot and coriander soup and a crusty baguette each.

"So, how did it go yesterday?" Stacey asked once they were alone. "Did you learn anything new?"

Lilly shook her head.

"Not really." She told Stacey about the argument she'd overheard between Laurel and Carl. "She's under a lot of stress at the moment. She realised she shouldn't have confronted him. But there's been something niggling at the back of my mind. Something I've seen or heard recently that's important, but I can't think what it is. It's infuriating."

"That's happened before, right? Don't think about it. It will come to you, eventually."

Stacey's phone pinged.

"That was a text from Abigail. She's at the bank and just seen another tour bus pull into the car-park."

"We'd better get our skates on then. It looks like it will be a busy afternoon."

ℓℓℓℓℓ

A COUPLE OF EVENINGS later, Lilly and Archie were walking through town on their way to the pub for an early dinner. "I see there's another new shop opening along the main street shortly," Archie said. "They've just bought some advertising space in the paper."

"Oh? What's it going to be? Anything interesting?"

Archie rolled his eyes. "A ladies' fashion brand I've never heard of. As if we haven't got enough of those already. There seems to be a new one launched every other day in this country, and, as far as I can tell, they all sell the same thing just at completely different prices. You know, for once I'd like to see a jolly good, upmarket menswear shop opening.

Something akin to those on Saville Row in London, where you can get a bespoke suit made by a tailor who has years of experience under his posh leather belt and knows what he's doing."

Lilly grinned. Archie really did love fine clothes.

"I suppose there are quite a few women's clothes shops in..." she stopped.

Archie carried on walking, then, realising she was no longer at his side, turned back.

"Lilly?"

But she was staring into space, completely oblivious to her surroundings. He knew better than to disturb her train of thought. She'd mentioned an elusive detail she was having trouble remembering.

Suddenly she whipped out her phone and began furiously prodding the screen. Scrolling desperately until she found what she was looking for. She strode toward him and thrust the phone forward for him to look at. It took a minute, but then he looked up.

"Is that..."

"Yes. Exactly the same as described."

Archie gulped. "Golly," he said, eyes on stalks.

"And look at this."

She scrolled and tapped some more and showed him another page. He read the information.

"Oh, well done, Lilly. At least that's one mystery solved. Although, this doesn't mean they killed Russell Davis."

"No, I know that. But you have to admit it is very suspicious, Archie."

"Oh, I agree. It certainly needs further investigation to find out why they did it."

"I think I know that reason. It's pretty obvious when you think about it. I've been a bit blind in that regard. It just depends whether it was the prelude to murder."

"Yes. Shocking, if it is. I never would have thought. What do you want to do now?"

"I need to see Bonnie. She needs to be updated on what we've found out. If this is our murderer, I also have a rough idea about how to set a trap."

*L*ILLY GLANCED AT her watch.

"I hope Bonnie's still at the station. It's only a five-minute walk from here. Otherwise, we'll have to get the car and drive to her house."

"I'll bet next month's salary she is in the office and neck deep in administration. She's a workaholic, Lilly. Especially when she's in the middle of a case."

Archie was proved right when the police detective answered on the third ring. She sounded tired and was catching up on the huge amount of paperwork the investigation had produced so far, but she was more than happy to see them both. Especially as Lilly informed her she had news that she thought was pertinent to the case.

She met them in the police station reception and took them to her office. Once she had her usual mug of strong black coffee in front of her, Bonnie turned to Lilly.

"You didn't tell me you were investigating the murder. Although I don't know why I'm surprised."

"It's not investigating, as such. I just talked to a few people, that's all. It's been on my mind constantly and I just thought I'd see what I could find out."

"Which in my book is called investigating."

They were interrupted by a knock at the door and a police constable put his head round the door.

"Sorry to bother you. I've just got a call about some youths in the park causing a bit of trouble, so I'm on my way down there."

"All right, thanks, Bob," Bonnie said. The constable disappeared, carefully closing the door behind him.

"His name is Bob?" Archie said. "As in Bobby?"

Bonnie smirked.

"Believe me, he's been the butt of several jokes ever since he arrived. But, he's taken it with good humour and given as good as he got. He's a popular member of the team and good at his job. But don't think changing the subject is going to let you off the hook, Archie Brown. I suppose you've been helping Lilly as well?"

Archie shrugged.

"A little."

"Well, as long as you haven't written anything in your articles that will scupper my investigation."

Archie held up both hands.

"Wouldn't dream of it without your say so, Bonnie. My pain threshold is akin to that of a toddler."

Bonnie smirked, but Lilly gasped.

"I've just remembered something else," she said. "Now I definitely know I'm on the right track."

"All right, Lilly," Bonnie said. "Start from the beginning and tell me what you've found out so far."

Lilly took a deep breath and began with her first visit to Felicity Russell to gather information. Bonnie remained silent, but nodded and took notes as she listened. Every so often she'd stop, raise an incredulous eyebrow and stare at Lilly, as though she couldn't believe what she was hearing.

"And then, just tonight, on the way to the pub, Archie said something that prompted a memory. It was that annoying little detail I just couldn't conjure up."

"But, you remembered it?"

"Yes. Eventually. Although I think I looked like a zombie for a while."

"You did," Archie said, nodding. "Definitely."

Lilly grinned at him, then turned back to her phone.

"Anyway, I found this."

Lilly handed her phone to Bonnie, who looked at the site already loaded.

"Okay. Anything else?"

"Yes."

Lilly retrieved her phone and, having found the page she was looking for, handed it back.

"Ah, I see," Bonnie said. "Yes, that's suspicious enough to warrant a conversation. But it doesn't mean murder."

"No. But, I have a plan, Bonnie. If it works, we could flush the murderer out. I truly think it's the same person. Why go to all that trouble otherwise? Plus, Archie talking about his aversion to pain just now made me remember something else."

She quickly brought the two of them up to date with another, far more important bit of information she'd discovered in the course of her conversations.

"Crikey, Lilly. You really have solved it. Hasn't she, Bonnie?" Archie said.

"Yes, it looks very much like it. Well done, Lilly. So, what's this plan you've got to trap them?"

Bonnie leaned back and sipped her coffee while Lilly explained what she had in mind. Ten minutes later, she'd finished and waited patiently for Bonnie to speak.

"Well," she said finally. "It's certainly not as hare-brained or dangerous as some of your past ideas have been. But are you absolutely sure?"

"I am, Bonnie. Ninety-nine percent, anyway."

"Okay. You've made a good case, actually. I'm inclined to agree with you. We'll need to make up a watertight excuse for us all to be there, though. We'll only get one crack at this, Lilly. Any skepticism or mistrust on their behalf and we'll show our hand. We might never get them then. Remember, this is all based on hearsay. We've no proof that would stand up in a court of law. What we need is a confession. I assume you're coming too, Archie?"

"Too right I am! I wouldn't miss it."

"Okay, let's thrash out some of the finer details."

"I don't think well on an empty stomach," Archie said. "And as we've missed our dinner at the pub, would you mind if we ordered something in?"

With fish and chips from the local shop ordered, and due to be delivered within the next ten minutes, they began in earnest to put together the trap which would expose the murderer once and for all.

It was going to be a long night.

Chapter Thirteen

THE FOLLOWING DAY, with as many i's dotted and t's crossed as they possibly could, Lilly and Archie were walking through Plumpton Mallet on their way to the town hall.

"Are you nervous?" Archie asked.

"You know, I am a bit, actually. Silly isn't it?"

"Of course not. We've done what we can in terms of working out potential scenarios and how we can react, but people are unpredictable, Lilly. Anything could happen."

"Yes, I feel much better now, Archie. Thank you.

Archie laughed and pulled her in for a brief hug.

"Sorry. But you know what I mean."

"I just hope there's no violence."

"Good grief, me too. But take solace in the fact Bonnie will be there. She could take down a man at ten paces and not break out in a sweat."

"I know. I've seen her in action on more than one occasion. It's a bit terrifying. Actually, that does make me feel a little better. Right, deep breaths, it's game on. Are you ready, Archie?"

"I am, Miss Tweed. Let's go and catch ourselves a killer!"

Inside, they approached the guard on duty. Once again, it was Jason.

"Hi, Lilly. Back again?"

"I am. And this time with a proper appointment to see the Mayor. Jason, this is Archie Brown, from the Plumpton Mallet Gazette. He's doing a piece on the Goodwin campaign and what happened to Councillor Davis."

"Righto. Let me check the list."

Jason reached for a clipboard hanging by the desk and, after flipping pages back and forth, looked up.

"I'm really sorry, Lilly, I can't see either of your names on today's list or listed for the next few days."

"What? Are you sure?" Archie asked. "A secretary at the office assured me she'd made it. Would you mind checking again?"

Jason did so, but his answer was the same.

"Jason," Lilly said. "There must be some misunderstanding. Perhaps someone forgot to put our names down? Is Laurel in?"

He looked at the staff log.

"Arrived a quarter of an hour ago. Do you want me to ring up and see what has happened?"

"If you don't mind, that would be a great help."

Lilly tried not to let her nervousness show while Jason was on the phone. Archie trod on her foot, and she grinned, realising she must have been subconsciously tapping it.

"Sorry, Lilly, she's not got you or Mr Brown on the list either," Jason said after speaking briefly with Laurel. "But she's on her way down to see you."

"Thanks, Jason."

Archie was just finishing up a phone call.

"Well, the girl at the office is adamant she made the appointment. Hopefully Miss Flowers can shed some light. Thanks for your help."

Lilly knew Archie's call hadn't been to his office, but to Bonnie, who was waiting nearby with one of her officers in order to turn up at exactly the right moment. That moment came a minute later when Laurel greeted them both in reception.

"Lilly, Archie, I'm so sorry. I don't know what happened, but it's not possible to see Mayor Goodwin today. Archie, do you know who you spoke to in the office here?"

Archie rubbed his chin, frowning.

"Sorry, Laurel, I don't. The secretary made it. I'm not even sure she gave me a name, actually. Just confirmed it was all organised for today."

"Lilly, Archie," a familiar voice said behind them. "What are you two doing here?"

"Oh, hi, Bonnie. We're trying to get in to see the mayor. Archie's secretary made an appointment, but it seems there's been an error and we're not on the list," Lilly said.

"Laurel," Bonnie said. "I need to see the mayor, too. I assume I don't need to be on the list?"

"No, Detective Phillips, of course not. Is there any news?"

Bonnie steered her away from the small group who had just entered. Lilly and Archie surreptitiously followed.

"Between you and me, I'm about to make an arrest for the murder of Russell Davis. I wanted to let you both know."

"Oh, that's excellent news. Who did it?"

"I'll tell you together, if you don't mind. Saves repeating it," Bonnie smiled. "Actually," she continued, turning to Lilly and Archie. "You two may as well come, too. As our local crime reporter, Archie, you can do a good write up for me. Make sure you give a glowing report of our town's police force and how swiftly and efficiently we have solved this case. That's all right, isn't it, Laurel?"

"Oh, er, yes, of course. Follow me."

Behind Laurel's back, Bonnie gave Lilly and Archie a wink. Part one of the plan was successfully completed.

❦

*T*HEY TOOK THE lift to the second floor and as soon as the door closed, Laurel turned to Bonnie. "Are you sure you can't tell me who did it, Detective Phillips? I'd like to be prepared before we see the mayor. It's bound to be a shock for him and he's under enough strain as it is. Was it Carl? I read somewhere that murders are usually committed by close family members. Is that right?"

"There are statistics that show that, yes," Bonnie replied with a friendly smile. "But I really would prefer to tell the mayor first, Laurel. There's a pecking order to stick to, as it were."

The lift pinged, and the door slid open.

"Yes, I understand. You need to tell the boss first. Follow me."

At the mayor's office she rapped on the door and pushed it open.

"Kenneth, I have Detective Phillips, Lilly Tweed, and Archie Brown to see you."

"Oh? All right, please, come in. I assume you have some news about Russell's death to tell me, Detective?"

"I have, Mayor."

"Well, take a seat and bring me up to date. Can I get you tea or coffee?"

The three of them shook their heads. Lilly and Archie took seats together near the wall, while Bonnie remained standing. Laurel also remained standing but moved, in a proprietorial gesture, nearer to the mayor.

"Mayor, I wanted to come myself to let you know I'm about to arrest someone for the murder of Russell Davis."

"Well, that is good news. Who is it, Detective?"

"Before I tell you, I'd like to hand over to Lilly. She's been instrumental in helping solve the case, and I want you to understand how she's helped us get to this stage."

Lilly crossed her fingers and silently prayed she was right. She was ninety-nine percent sure she was, but the additional one percent was a bit of a nagging worry. Out of the corner of her eye, she saw Archie open his notebook and draw a smiley face. His proximity calmed her. She took a deep breath. The moment had come. It was time for phase two of the plan, and it could either go as she hoped or completely pear-shaped.

"By all means, Lilly. Carry on," Mayor Goodwin said encouragingly, leaning forward with eagerness.

"A few days ago, Mayor Goodwin, I went to visit your wife."

"Wait, a minute. Stop. What? You spoke to Rose? But why? She wasn't present on the night it happened. She doesn't even live in Plumpton Mallet anymore."

"The reason I went was because I was getting conflicting messages as to why she left in the first place, and I wanted to get a definitive answer."

"I spoke to you in confidence, Lilly. Besides, what on earth has the state of my marriage got to do with this murder?" the mayor asked indignantly. He turned. "Bonnie, this really is out of order. Poking into my private life is well outside the bounds of professionalism I come to expect from our police force."

"Believe me, I do understand why you're annoyed, Ken, but if you let Lilly finish, she'll explain how it fits into the case."

"Thank you, Bonnie," Lilly said. "When I went to visit her, she told me she left because she'd found out you were having an affair."

"An affair? But that's... are you serious? But that's absolutely ridiculous. I've never had, nor would I ever have, an affair. Rose was, and still is, the love of my life. I was devastated when she left. Dear, god. Where did she get that idea from? And why didn't she tell me?"

"She said she'd found some women's underwear in your bag when you returned from a trip." Lilly watched the man's jaw drop. "She left it out in an obvious place in the hope you'd instigate a conversation, but you never did. She realised then you were having an affair, but rather than destroy your reputation, which would most likely lose you your job, she chose to go quietly. She knew how much being mayor meant to you and how hard you'd worked to remain in office."

"I truly have no idea what you're talking about?" Kenneth said, stunned.

He got up on shaking legs, looking grey and utterly bewildered, and approached the oak sideboard, intending to pour himself a glass of water. Laurel got there first.

"Let me, Kenneth."

Once the mayor had taken several deep gulps and the colour was beginning to return to his face, Laurel turned to Lilly.

"Are you happy now? This is a dreadful shock and, quite frankly, I can't see what this has to do with Carl murdering his uncle."

"But Carl didn't murder his uncle, Laurel," Lilly said.

"But the detective said..."

Bonnie shook her head.

"No, I didn't. You heard what you wanted to hear, Laurel. Recent statistics actually show male victims are most likely to be murdered either by strangers or by people in the work place."

"What exactly is going on here?" Mayor Goodwin said, glancing between Bonnie and Lilly. "Do you know anything about this supposed underwear my wife found? And do you actually know who killed Russell?"

"I think Laurel can answer your first question, Mayor," Bonnie said.

The mayor turned to his assistant.

"Laurel?"

"Me? Why would I know anything?"

"Because it was you who hid the garment in the Mayor's luggage on a trip, you both took to London," Lilly replied.

"No," Laurel gasped. But she could see the jig was up.

"When you came to book the fundraising event, I remembered Abigail and I complimented you on your outfit. Your reply was that you also had the matching underwear. It all came from your mother's boutique. A quick search on-line brought up the shop in question and I found the exact same lingerie Rose Goodwin described to me. The about section on the website listed your mother as the proprietor. They're an exclusive brand, Laurel. They couldn't have come from anyone else."

While Lilly was speaking, the mayor had edged away from Laurel and was now back behind his desk. He stared at his assistant with a mix of horror and confusion.

"But why, Laurel? Why would you do such a dreadful thing?" he said.

Laurel shook her head and began to cry. Wracking sobs that were painful to listen to.

"Because she's in love with you," Lilly answered softly. "I believe she thought by removing your wife she could slowly integrate herself into, not only your work life, but your private one as well. Proving herself indispensable and a tower of strength and support, eventually her feelings for you would be reciprocated. That the two of you would marry, and as you were mayor, she would become mayoress. She envisaged you both running the town together. Plumpton Mallet's power couple, perhaps."

"But, that's ridiculous. Rose is the only woman I've ever loved. I don't want anyone else." He suddenly got up. "I need to speak with her. I have to put this right."

"Perhaps you could wait, Ken," Bonnie said. "There's still the matter of Russell's murder to discuss."

"Russell. Yes, of course. But I think Laurel should leave. Quite frankly, I no longer want her here."

Laurel looked at the mayor as though she'd been punched. She reeled back, suddenly realising her plans and subterfuge had been for nothing. Before she could speak, Lilly jumped up.

"I don't think that will be possible, I'm afraid. You see, it was Laurel who also murdered Russell Davis."

⟨ℓℓℓℓ⟩

THE WHOLE ROOM fell silent as everyone turned to Laurel. Lilly was holding her breath, hoping that her plan would unfold as she expected. Mayor Goodwin was the first to speak.

"Dear god, Laurel. Tell me it isn't true? Tell me you didn't murder an innocent man?"

"Innocent?" Laurel suddenly shrieked. "How can you say that after all he's done? Russell Davis wasn't innocent. He was intent on destroying a town you had so lovingly built up and made a success. He was going to ruin everything you'd achieved! Please, Ken, can't you understand? I did it for us."

"Us?" Ken Goodwin replied incredulously. "Hell's teeth, Laurel, what on earth are you talking about? There is no 'us.' There never has been and never will be."

"But I love you. Don't you realise that? Imagine what we can do together. We could really make Plumpton Mallet the best town in the North of England, if not the entire country. Everyone will flock to see us."

"This isn't love, Laurel. It's an obsession. You murdered a man for crying out loud! And for what reason? Because you disagreed with his ideas for the town? And why attempt to frame his nephew? What had Carl done to wrong you so badly?"

"It wasn't just me Carl insulted, Kenneth! He was rude and insufferable. He denigrated you at every opportunity. Said you were too old to be in the job and it was time someone younger took over. He'd call me at all hours wanting favours or my help to get you to see sense and retire. The man is an imbecile and should never have been in such a high position in the first place. He deserved everything he got. You should be grateful to me for getting rid of Russell and helping to clear the way so you can continue to do the job you are so good at."

This was all Lilly had been hoping for and Bonnie needed no further admission of guilt. She stepped forward.

"Laurel Flowers, I'm arresting you for the murder of Russell Davis."

She took Laurel by the arm and opened the door. She'd already arranged for a constable to be standing outside, and after reading Laurel her rights, handed her over. Lilly breathed a sigh of relief.

"**I** APOLOGISE FOR THE drama involved Ken," Bonnie said, once the office door was closed, and the conversation was again private. "But it was the only way we could get Laurel to admit what she'd done in front of witnesses."

"I'm absolutely staggered. It was Laurel all along? Dear God. Not only has she ruined my marriage, but she's taken the life of a colleague and tried to put the blame on someone else. She can't be in her right mind." He shook his head sadly, then looked at Lilly. "How exactly did you piece it all together?"

Lilly shrugged. "By simply talking to people and finding where the details didn't add up or contradicted. Once I'd established it was Laurel who had planted the underwear, along with the most probable reason for her doing so, my next thought was the murder must have something to do with you. Laurel has always been over-attentive and protective where you're concerned. In almost every conversation I've ever had with her, her concern for you was the main topic of conversation. Initially, I thought it was because she was being an excellent assistant, but, like you said, it quickly began to look more like an obsession. I knew she didn't like Carl at all. She'd already mentioned that to me, so I then began to look at ways in which she could have framed him. The big one, obviously, was how she could plant the murder weapon in his car."

"Yes. I wondered about that. What did you find out?"

"I was privy to a nasty argument between them both at the wake. It actually was Laurel, in no uncertain terms, accusing Carl of murder. I think that was to throw everyone off the scent. Especially me as I was talking to anyone I could think of and cement it in people's minds that he was the guilty party. In hindsight, I believe she was all too aware I was in the powder room at the time and couldn't help but overhear. But she made an obvious mistake. Which stupidly I didn't pick up at the time."

"And what was that?" Ken Goodwin asked.

"She told Carl she knew the knife had been found in his car because it had been reported in the paper. As the only crime reporter, it would have been up to Archie to write the article."

"But I didn't write it," Archie continued. "I was under strict instructions from Detective Phillips not to publish any information that would jeopardise the investigation. The knife being found in Carl's car was germane to the enquiry and would never have been written about in the paper. Not least because it could very well have caused a riot or a witch hunt for a potentially innocent man."

"So," Lilly said, taking up the story again. "The only way Laurel could have known about it was..."

"If she'd put it there herself," Ken Goodwin finished for her, nodding wearily. "Yes. I see. So how did she do it?"

"After she left, I stayed with Carl for a minute to check he was all right. He really was in a bad way. He mentioned to me he'd taken her home one evening after her car had broken down close to his house."

"Do you think her car really broke down?" Archie asked.

"I can't say for sure, but I doubt it. No doubt there'll be an examination of her vehicle. Is that right, Bonnie?"

"It is."

"So, what do you think happened when Carl took her home?" Ken asked.

"I don't know for sure, because I wasn't there, but this is what I think. She knocked on his door and explained the situation. Perhaps when Carl went to get his coat, she took his keys. Not being able to find them, he took the spare instead. Or she took the spare, and he was none the wiser, as it wasn't the one he used frequently. Once free, Laurel made a copy of the key and used it the night of the fundraiser to put the murder weapon in his car. Then, sometime later, she'll have put his keys back somewhere he would find them and think he'd left them there himself."

"Wait," Bonnie said. "When we questioned him in the car park on the night, he said he was always losing his keys."

Lilly nodded. "Yes. It will have been at the forefront of his mind because it had happened so recently."

"Returning the keys to his desk drawer wouldn't have taken much either," Ken Goodwin said. "His office is in this building next to Russell's."

"But how do you think she'll have known where to find his keys in the first place, Lilly?" Archie asked.

"Most likely he did what Russell did. I think he had some hero worship as far as his uncle was concerned, so emulating his habits would have been almost second nature. He might not have been aware he was even doing it. When I went to visit Felicity, I noticed a crystal bowl on the hall table filled with keys. I do the same thing when I get home. Close the door and chuck my house and car keys in a bowl on the hall table. That way they're always at hand, close to the front door and the car outside. And I'm not spending ages trying to remember where I put them."

Archie nodded. "I do the same thing. It's a habit you get into without even thinking about it. It would have been quite easy for Laurel to quickly pick them up and put them in her bag without Carl noticing, wouldn't it?"

"Absolutely. And, who knows, it might not have been her first visit to his house. She could have seen them there at any time and mentally filed away the information."

"You know, if you think about it, this whole thing has been my fault," Ken Goodwin said.

"Why has it? Did you encourage Laurel's belief that you felt the same way she did?" Bonnie asked. "Flirted with her, led her on and made her think there was a future for you together as a couple?"

"Good lord, no!" was the shocked reply. "I had no idea how she felt. I treated her the same way I treat all my staff. With respect and appreciation for the jobs they do. But I never got too close. Quite the opposite."

"Then it's not your fault, Ken. The only one to blame is Laurel. You're not responsible for her actions. That's down to her. Now, if you'll excuse me, I have a case to wrap up."

"I'll come with you," Lilly said. "Archie?"

"Actually, I just want to have a quick word with Ken. I'll meet you at the coffee shop over the road. Is that all right?"

"Of course it is. Mayor, I really am sorry about how all this has turned out. But Bonnie is right. Don't waste your time or energy blaming yourself for what Laurel did. That's a fast-track way to a breakdown. Concentrate on looking forward and embracing the positive things in your life. This will all blow over soon."

"Thank you, Lilly. Goodbye, Bonnie. And well done."

"*W*ELL, THAT WENT better than I expected," Bonnie said as she and Lilly stood outside the town hall. "Well done, my friend."

Lilly grinned. "Thanks, Bonnie. I must say I'm so relieved it went how I'd hoped. My heart was in my mouth several times."

"Yours and mine both. Well, that's another case solved. How many is it now? Seven or eight? Yes, eight, I think."

"Crikey, is it really that many?"

"Oh yes. You're the Miss Marple of the North, Lilly. I think half the tourists we get in town now only come to gawk at you and to ask about the new murder tour."

"What?" squeaked Lilly. "You can't be serious!"

"Oh, yes," Bonnie replied, dead-panned. "The tourist information staff are all on board, and I believe Fred and Stacey are putting together a map of all the crime scenes, along with the list of suspects and victims. And of course, all the clues you used to solve the crimes."

Lilly just stared at her friend in horror. This was the worst thing she could imagine, not to mention it was in really poor taste. Suddenly Bonnie, unable to keep a straight face any longer, cracked up. Hands on her stomach as she guffawed so loudly, several people stopped to stare and two approached to ask if she was all right.

"Bonnie Phillips! That was a mean trick!" Lilly said, then couldn't help but join in with the laughter. "Wow, you really had me going there for a minute."

"I know," Bonnie giggled. "But it was worth it to see the look on your face."

"So, moving on. Do you know why Archie wanted to speak privately with the mayor?"

"No idea. Probably about the article he's writing, I would think. I'll catch up with you soon, Lilly. I have an important interview to do."

Lilly waved Bonnie goodbye, with the words 'I'll get you back one day,' and after a lull in the traffic, wandered across the road to the End of the Line coffee shop. It seemed ages ago since she'd last been here, waiting in the exact same place for Kenneth Goodwin to finish work. She was nursing her second large cappuccino when Archie finally joined her.

"You were gone a while. What was that all about?" Lilly asked.

"Oh, you know. A conversation da uomo a uomo."

Lilly laughed. "This is because we're in an Italian coffee shop, I suppose."

Archie grinned and nodded. "Probably."

"So, what was the subject of your man-to-man conversation? Besides the obvious."

Archie took his phone out of his pocket and put it on the table.

"I recorded the whole meeting on my phone, Lilly."

"Good grief, Mr Brown. Is this you embracing the twenty-first century at last?"

"I know. It's amazing, isn't it? Who would have thought? But, back to the point, if you don't mind, Miss Tweed."

"Sorry, Mr Brown, do carry on."

"This whole thing has been an absolute shock to the system for Ken. I thought he might need a friendly ear. Not to sound sexist or anything, but I felt a bit of support from a man's perspective might help."

"And did it?"

"Oh, yes. He's absolutely cut to the quick that Rose thinks he had an affair. But, he was worried if he told her what really happened it would sound too far-fetched, and a convenient excuse. So I told him I'd recorded everything. Don't worry, I'd already informed Bonnie of my intention and she was agreeable. In fact, I've already sent the file to her by e-mail. It's amazing what you can do on a phone nowadays. But I digress. During the conversation, Ken knew nothing about my recording it. He was as candid as he could be, and his innocence flowed off him in waves. He really had no idea at all what Laurel had done, and it was obvious to anyone listening how horrified he was. He was devastated that his wife thought he'd had an affair and immediately wanted to make amends. You heard him, Lilly. He really was heartbroken. Like he said, she is and remains the love of his life. But, more to the point, if she was able to listen to the recording, it would be obvious to Rose, too."

"Oh, Archie. You called and played it to her?" Lilly said, suddenly feeling emotional.

"I did. Well, actually, we both did. I was happy for Ken to do it privately, but he insisted."

"And what happened?"

"She was shocked, as you can imagine. She'd always thought Laurel was an excellent PA. She had no idea she'd been harbouring romantic feelings for her husband. Anyway, the upshot is Ken is going over to Timbleby this evening to take Rose out for dinner and a heart to heart chat."

"Oh, Archie, that really is such good news."

"And there's another bit. Ken has decided to retire. I think he's realised there's more to life than work and what time he's got left he wants to spend with his wife."

"She did mention to me how little she saw of him because of his obligation to the job. I think once their sons had grown and left home, she felt lonely and rudderless. Just drifting, with no idea where she was headed or what she wanted to do. And what does Ken feel about Felicity becoming Mayor?"

"He's all for it. He didn't agree with Russell's ideas, but he's convinced she will do what's best for the town and the residents. He told me the two of them have actually had a few chats in private recently and her love for Plumpton Mallet is the same as his own. He thinks she'll do a very good job. He'll be making his announcement and giving her his public support over the coming days."

"And you've got your article."

"More than one, I think. Now, how about some food? Or do you have to get back to the shop?"

"I think I can spare an hour," Lilly replied and went to get the menu.

Chapter Fourteen

"SO YOU WENT into that meeting without really knowing it was Laurel who'd killed Russell?" Stacey said, eyes wide in amazement.

It was the day after Laurel's arrest and Lilly was back in the shop with Stacey and James. The first article had appeared in that morning's paper, courtesy of Archie, so she was free to 'spill the beans' as Stacey put it.

"I was ninety-nine percent sure. But it was a bit nerve-wracking."

"I can't believe it was her! Way to go, Lilly! Another one solved."

Lilly laughed. "And let's hope that's the last one."

The phone rang and James went to answer it just as the doorbell tinkled. In walked a large bouquet of stunning flowers, behind which the delivery driver stood.

"These aren't from me either," he said with a grin.

"Oh, hello again," Lilly said, laughing, remembering their last conversation.

"Ooo, how gorgeous! Who are they from?" Stacey asked, leaning forward to smell the fragrance from the coral and orange roses. "Archie hasn't been upsetting you again, has he?"

"No, of course not."

Lilly plucked the card from the centre and read it.

"It's from Felicity, Josephine, and Carl, thanking me for solving the case. How lovely of them."

"I've got a message for you, Lilly," James said, waving a note. "Apparently, the organisers of this year's Amateur Artist competition would like you on board as a judge."

"Crikey. Really?"

"It's official then," Stacey said, nodding sagely. "Lilly Tweed, super sleuth, has hit the big time. Face it, Lilly, you're a celebrity now."

"Gosh, I hope not," she said, shuddering as she remembered Bonnie's practical joke. "But being a judge for the art competition sounds wonderful."

"Are you going to do it?" James asked.

"Yes, I think I am. There are a lot of superb artists in Plumpton Mallet. It will be nice to get more involved this year."

"You never know, there might be another case to solve," Stacey said.

Lilly rolled her eyes. She very much doubted it.

But that's another story.

THE TEA EMPORIUM IS ON-LINE!

Here you can find all Lilly's favourite health teas, china, gifts for tea and book lovers, tableware and more. All in one place. Including Earl Grey's favourite bed!

If you want to know more about the products mentioned in Lilly's shop and to purchase your own, just visit THE TEA EMPORIUM at jnewwrites.com and read the reviews from Lilly and the rest of the characters. Even Earl has something to say!

From looking for that perfect teapot to finding ideas and inspiration to help plan and host your own Afternoon Tea or event, there's something for everyone.

Stacey will be updating the page with new products regularly, so be sure to pop back to see what she has added.

If there's something you're looking for which isn't listed, just visit the about page on the website jnewwrites.com and let us know.

If you enjoyed *High Tea Low Opinions*, the eighth book in the Tea & Sympathy series, please leave a review on Amazon. It really does help readers find the book.

ABOUT THE AUTHOR

J. New is the author of *THE YELLOW COTTAGE VINTAGE MYSTERIES,* traditional English whodunits with a twist, set in the 1930's. Known for their clever humour as well as the interesting slant on the traditional murder mystery, they have all achieved Bestseller status on Amazon.

J. New also writes two contemporary cozy crime series:

THE TEA & SYMPATHY series featuring Lilly Tweed, former newspaper Agony Aunt now purveyor of fine teas at The Tea Emporium in the small English market town of Plumpton Mallet. Along with a regular cast of characters, including Earl Grey the shop cat.

THE FINCH & FISCHER series featuring mobile librarian Penny Finch and her rescue dog Fischer. Follow them as they dig up clues and sniff out red herrings in the six villages and hamlets that make up Hampsworthy Downs.

Jacquie was born in West Yorkshire, England. She studied art and design and after qualifying began work as an interior designer, moving onto fine art restoration and animal portraiture before making the decision to pursue her lifelong ambition to write. She now writes full time and lives with her partner of twenty-two years, two dogs and five cats, all of whom she rescued.

If you would like to be kept up to date with new releases from J. New, you can sign up to her *Reader's Group* on her website www.jnewwrites.com You will also receive a link to download the free e-book, *The Yellow Cottage Mystery*, the short-story prequel to The Yellow Cottage Vintage Mystery series.

.

Printed in Great Britain
by Amazon